Fit

SAMMY WRIGHT

SHEFFIELD – LONDON – NEW YORK

First published in 2021 by And Other Stories
Sheffield – London – New York
www.andotherstories.org

1 3 5 7 9 8 6 4 2

ISBN: 9781913505127
eBook ISBN: 9781913505134

Editor: Jeremy M. Davies; Copy-editor: Bella Bosworth; Proofreader: Gesche Ipsen; Text designed and set in Albertan Pro and Syntax by Tetragon, London; Cover Design: Jon Gray. Printed and bound on acid-free, age-resistant Munken Premium by CPI Limited, Croydon, UK.

A catalogue record for this book is available from the British Library.

And Other Stories gratefully acknowledge that our work is supported using public funding by Arts Council England.

For Mum, for the job you did,
and for the people still doing it

And for Clare

'Early tomorrow morning we will take the children out into the forest to where it is the thickest; there we will light a fire for them, and give each of them one more piece of bread, and then we will go to our work and leave them alone. They will not find the way home again, and we shall be rid of them.'

'And you,' he said to Cinderella, *'what do you want?'*

ONCE

Here's Rose.

Most people say her eyes are too far apart. When she's bored, like now, she wraps her legs (in the yellow leggings) round each other, one foot hooked around the other ankle. She does the same with her hands, twisting them so the wrists cross. She can feel the fingers on her left hand touch the skin on the wrist of her right.

'What did one hat say to the other?' she says. She's eleven, but she often seems younger.

Aaron doesn't notice. He's eight, and is sitting on a low wall. His hair is thin and blond and clipped almost to baldness. He wears her old T-shirt. It says 'Princess' in purple glitter.

The two of them are outside the shop, and their mother is inside. Rose can feel the damp pavement through her sock. She switches feet, and, balancing, reaches her yellow leg out to prod Aaron with a toe.

'What did one hat say to the other?' she says again.

Aaron's face skews into a bony grin.

'You wait here. I'll go on a head,' says Rose.

Aaron says, 'Good one.'

They always say, 'Good one.'

'Your turn,' says Rose.

Aaron's eyes drift up in thought.

Rose peers through the glass. She likes the way her own reflection sits like a ghost over the people inside. She can see them moving past clothes, toasters, loose shoes in buckets, pick 'n' mix. She shifts a little so her face floats over a woman in a bright blue dress.

'Oh!'

Aaron half rises from his seat on the wall. His limbs lurch, puppet-like.

'What did one butt cheek say to the other?' he shouts.

'I don't know,' says Rose.

'If we stick together we can stop this shit!'

Aaron cackles, a high, raw, dizzy sound that spills out of his slight frame. He's so skinny you can clearly see where the skull dips in at his temples.

'Good one,' says Rose. She smiles at him.

Aaron falls silent, a look of wonder at the brilliance of that joke still on his face.

Rose switches feet again. Through the window she can see glimpses of her mother, a heel, the edge of a red coat as she rounds an aisle. When she dresses up like this, she seems like a different person.

At home, they have a magazine. Rose reads it, every night. She always looks on the back cover first. The girl there is long limbed, red hooded. Beside her a wolf, sleek, pale eyed. Trees, fingering the darkness, and a moon, a penny dropped on black velvet. She has a dream that feels like the picture, a dream of night as thick and rich as chocolate.

The shop door slams.

'Rose!'

Her mother's voice hisses in her ear. She feels thin fingers grip her cheek and then they press something in at her mouth. For a moment she smells the sour faggy musk of her mother's unwashed hands, and then the sugar hits, a bright, glorious fizz of cola.

'Now, quick.'

Aaron jumps up and runs off ahead. Rose hurries after him in her stockinged feet. Her mouth is filled with saliva. She feels light and dizzy. She thinks that there has never been a better taste in all the world.

'Did you get them?' she shouts back to her mother.

'Yes!'

Rose runs faster, lighter, the balls of her feet aching.

That's how it starts. It's always the same. There are rules, and when you break them, somewhere out there in the forest the wolf pricks up his ears, and the story begins.

RAGS

Three years later.

Beyond the end of the estate is the bridge. Where the bridge crosses the river, the path passes under the arch. When spring comes, when they are fourteen, this is where Alisha teaches Dillon to smoke.

Dillon takes the cigarette from the packet. He holds it tentatively between his finger and thumb. His face is white and round, pasty pale and featureless with youth. His eyes are pale too, a soft grey under faded blond eyebrows.

Oni laughs. 'It won't bite,' she says.

Oni's face is also plump and young, but she is as black as he is white, a proper rich blue-black. Alisha is somewhere in between, dark with fake tan and foundation, her eyelashes heavy, false and beautiful.

Alisha takes the cigarette off him. She puts it between her shiny lips and lights it. Her cheeks suck in.

'Here,' she says.

The end of the cigarette is on fire. Dillon can see the smoke.

He takes it. He almost touches her fingers, bright with blue gel nails. He can feel the air between them. He lifts the cigarette to his mouth. He catches a sticky, enchanting hint of strawberry lip gloss on the filter.

He blushes, and inhales deeply.

After he's finished coughing, he stays down, head between his knees. He spits. Sticks his tongue out.

'Blah,' he says. 'That's fucking rank.'

Alisha catches Oni's eye. 'Pass it,' she says, reaching out. She draws, lets the smoke drift casually over her face. She passes it to Oni, who smokes it down then flicks the butt perfectly into the grass.

They step out from under the arch and head on up the path. After the bridge, the trees gather round the river. The path muddies, and roots curl across its surface. Everything is worn. The trunks by the path are etched with names and dates, the weeds rich with urine. Cider bottles gather in pockets at the base of wide-branched trees.

There are witches hiding here, if you look.

When Dillon was six, he saw them from the bridge. He peered over with his mother into the twilight, and the shadows cackled with laughter under wreaths of cigarette smoke. Witches and beasts and love and lost children.

Every town has a wood like this. Maybe the trees are streetlamps, or goalposts, or concrete pillars wrapped in chicken wire, but there is always a place like this, where teenagers step out, alone, into adulthood, finding out the rules for themselves.

The girls lead the way. Dillon watches. His mouth tastes awful, but the day is high and bright. The girls wear the same clothes. Jeans, trainers, puffy bomber jackets with huge fur-lined hoods. He thinks they look amazing. It's hard to say what makes them so amazing, but they are. They know things he can't dream of.

When they talk to each other it makes no sense.
'She said she was a sket.'
'Well she is a fucking sket. I don't even care if it's blue.'
'I just think she should know herself.'
'What's your name? *Barbara*?'
Then they laugh, long and hard, doubling up theatrically.
Sometimes they talk to Dillon.
'Who have you kissed?'
'Have you kissed Ceri?'
'He's never kissed Ceri!'
'Have you kissed Rose?'
'Don't be fucking disgusting!'
Alisha frowns at him. 'You haven't kissed Rose, have you?'
'No,' he says, affronted.
'What's wrong with Rose?' says Oni, eyes sparkling.
'Shut up,' says Alisha. 'You can smell her period.'
Oni roars with delight.
At a turn in the path they find some glass bottles and break them. Dillon throws some stones. He jumps to catch a low branch and pulls himself upside down. They laugh again.
Oni looks him in the eye and says, 'Do you want to kiss me?'
He can't stop himself looking to Alisha. She grins, her eyes wide and expressionless.
He kisses Oni. He moves towards her face, and he thinks he's about to kiss her, and he imagines that he's about to kiss her, and then he is, and it takes him by surprise that it's happening there, on his face, with his lips and her lips, wet and strange, and not just in his head after all.
Her mouth moves open and closed, and his does too, and

her tongue slips inside, so his does too, and he feels like he is balancing on something.

They stop. Alisha claps.

One day they go farther. Dillon, and Oni, and Alisha. They walk beyond the well-worn paths, and take the turning that climbs higher up the sides of the valley. There is less rubbish here. The weeds seem cleaner. The path winds around the trees, rather than pushing a straight line through them. Alisha sings a song. It's one that they hear on the radio. Her voice is in tune, heartfelt. Dillon listens, astonished.

Oni holds Dillon's hand. They have kissed three times now. She might be his girlfriend. Her face is round, plump, black. It might also be beautiful. It's so hard to tell these things. If he was black too, he might be able to tell.

The woods are dirty, and he is alone, and scared. The woods are beautiful, and he's in love.

There is magic, and there is none.

His shoes thicken in the mud.

Alisha showers, uses the products her mum bought her. She dries her hair, stands in front of the mirror. She moves her head carefully, one side to another. She smiles, frowns. Widens her eyes to look at their pink corners. Leans close to look for spots. Draws a careful line around an eye and feels a lift, giddy and slight and sweet, like a step into a well-fitting dress, like someone laughing at one of her jokes.

At breakfast her mum circles her warily.

'What are you having?'

'Juice.'

'Just juice?'
'Yes just juice. Why?'
'No reason.'
'Stop it.'
'Stop what?'
'Stop having a go.'
'How did I have a go?'
They pause.
'Are you allowed jeans?'
'If they're black,' she lies.
'What's on today, then?'
'School.'
'Alisha.'
'What? It's the same every day.'

Dillon looks in the mirror too. He clenches his jaw and frowns at himself. He lowers his brows farther, until he's squinting. He curls his lip. Then his face clears. There isn't much for a boy to do, other than hope. He hopes his smooth pink cheeks will darken with stubble, or harden into an angular jawline. He hopes he might get chest hair, or grow taller and more muscular. He imagines it happening, like in 'Beauty and the Beast'.

He frowns again, as if he's in pain. That's part of it. You have to be hurt into manliness. Sometimes he dreams of being beaten up. On the corners of his exercise books he draws thickset faces, bald headed, broken nosed.

He checks his pubes.

Maybe a girl will touch him one day. He can't quite imagine it, though.

. . .

Another day, they are coming back down towards the bridge. The path runs into a dense block of shadow under the stone arch. As they get closer, the light from the other side picks out the legs of two figures standing in the darkness.

A faint wisp of smoke curls out from under the arch.

Alisha and Oni walk quickly on. Dillon follows, slower.

One of the figures is Aaron. No one else has trousers that flap around stick-thin legs like that. No one else stands as if interrupted mid-turn. His wonky limbs have a frozen grace to them, like crooked branches.

Next to him, feet planted wide, is a boy who is everything Aaron is not. Where Aaron's features are delicate, but disturbingly ugly, this boy has a rough, thuggish beauty. Aaron looks like he might snap in a high wind, but the boy next to him is iron-hard, solid as the arch above them.

He smokes like he knows how.

'Can I get a tab?' asks Oni. Her eyes catch the low light under the arch; bright and eager against the shadowed stone.

The boy holds one out. He offers the packet to Alisha as well. Not to Dillon.

Alisha and Oni draw a cigarette each. They light them. Dillon waits. He doesn't want one, but he doesn't want to be the person not smoking one. The boy draws on his cigarette, then opens his mouth to let the smoke coil out gently. Wiry cords of adult muscle knot his shoulders.

His nose is broken.

'You're new, aren't you?' asks Alisha. 'Your name's Jack, isn't it?'

He nods.

The girls are ignoring Dillon. He looks at Aaron. Aaron's smoking too, even though he's only eleven, but he does it in a different way. He holds his hand by his mouth at all times, and when he draws, his cheeks grow deep hollows. In that moment, you can see that the skull underneath is not symmetrical. His cheekbones are huge, but they are not the same, and his jaw moves in a way that is somehow not right.

Dillon shivers.

'Easy, mate.'

Jack's voice has a rasping, mocking quality. It isn't a question, but it needs an answer. Dillon shrugs, his face carefully blank apart from a slightly pained frown. Jack laughs. When he laughs, he throws his head back, opens his mouth wide. His body moves too. The arms swing, the feet plant themselves restlessly, over and over, in the same spot.

'Which one's your girlfriend?'

Dillon goes white. He shrugs again.

'He's just our friend,' says Alisha.

They walk back into town together. Dillon walks beside Aaron, Jack in front with the girls.

Dillon watches Alisha. Aaron watches Jack.

A week later, on the way back from visiting his mum at the hospital, Dillon gets off the bus at the bridge. He stands above where the path passes beneath. He can smell the grain of cigarette smoke. As his eyes adjust he can see someone in the shadow below. Two figures, one kneeling. Then a bright dot glows, smoke is drawn in, and he sees Jack's wicked face looking up at him while Oni fumbles at his crotch.

Dillon steps back. The river curves away towards the forest. The sun is low, the light red.

This town is stone, mostly. Rows of stone terraces nestled in a valley. A market street, a town hall, shops with the names painted on stone lintels. If you follow the river down, you're soon in the forest. But stick to the road, and you enter the twenty-first century. Over the bridge, past the old stone warehouse, beyond the sharp grey rows of new houses, sits the industrial estate with its hangar-like supermarket and tile and carpet merchants, grouped around double roundabouts and unmarked roads.

But go farther still, and you're out. The land rises, the valley deepens, the tops beckon. Floating on the long crests of purple moor are islands of stone, like blunt-headed breaching whales, circled by the thick runnels of peat-cut tracks. Up there, you can sit in the nook of a rock and see nothing but sky.

The beach is an hour away in the other direction. The first time Rose and Aaron are taken there, they arrive late, as the sun is setting over the wide bay. They stand watching everything carefully. Then something catches Aaron and he runs, arms at his sides, hands in his pockets, his skinny torso wobbling and his head down against the wind and the sand, his coat flapping against a body that almost isn't there.

Rose stays back, watching her brother. Her foot is twisted round her ankle, her wrists interlock. The sea is big. Aaron is small against it. It's flatter than she thought it would be.

She imagines she is a rubber band, twisted tight. She tenses, then releases, flinging herself wide into a sudden, gawky pirouette. She staggers a little, then spins again.

Graeme watches too. He is heavy, greying and still, carrying a weariness with him even here.

Jack doesn't care about the beach. He's been living with them for a month. The sea isn't new to him. On the way to the caravan, he promised them all it would be shit. Since they arrived, he's stood beside Graeme, poking the sand with his foot.

But he raises his head now and watches Rose. They're the same age. He watches, then shouts, a huge, incoherent roar. He runs at her. Rose turns sharply. He pounds into her, a full-body tackle, and the two fall. Rose shrieks.

'Jack!' shouts Graeme.

Aaron is a few hundred yards away. He comes running back, twisting and flapping. Jack and Rose roll on the ground. Graeme gets to them first, pulls at Jack's hoody. The two of them are flailing, sandy. Rose flings her head back, and Graeme sees with a shock her wild grin of delight just as Aaron hurtles up and flings himself onto Jack. Jack rolls, Graeme stumbles, and they all go down.

'Stop!' roars Graeme.

And they do.

They are on the sand, damp seeping into their clothes. The sea is wide, the sky wider. They half lie, half sit, in a heap. Jack's leg rests across Rose, Aaron is leaning against Graeme.

Graeme can hear their breathing.

'OK,' he says.

They wait.

'OK,' he says again.

Later, in the caravan, Graeme tells them a new joke.

'Why do seagulls fly over the sea?'

'I don't know,' says Aaron.

'Because if they flew over the bay, they'd be bagels.'

Aaron cackles. He picks Graeme's phone up.

Rose has three magazines spread out on the pull-out bed in front of her – *Vogue, Cosmopolitan* and *Take a Break.* Caz, the social worker, brings them every time she visits. She's large, like Graeme. Maybe fat. She and Rose sit, side by side, carefully turning the pages. When she leaves, Rose cuts the pictures they were looking at out of the magazines and puts them up in her room. She cuts out adverts for perfume and clothes and shots from red-carpet photocalls and feature interviews with beautiful people and adverts for furniture and kitchenware and limited-edition figurines of shepherdesses. The pictures cover the whole wall now.

In the caravan, Rose turns the pages slowly. Faces smile back. Her brows draw in, an expression of faint puzzlement on her face. Page after page, slick and mysterious.

Jack is outside. The football makes a steady thunk on the wall. Every time it hits, the caravan shudders.

Aaron puts Graeme's phone down on the table and clambers over to sit on the bed by Rose. He looks over her shoulder.

Thunk.

'Jack!'

Thunk.

Graeme stands up and goes to the door. 'Ball,' he says.

Jack hands him the ball. He follows Graeme back into the caravan. He stands in the middle of the main room, kicking his toe gently against the edge of the kitchen cabinet. Then he goes to Rose.

He climbs onto the bed with care on the other side of Rose. Aaron, Rose, Jack. Their shoulders touching, their feet stretched out. The magazine on Rose's lap.

Graeme watches from the table.

'Do you think they're all rich?' asks Jack.

They look intently at the page.

'Yes,' says Rose, after a moment. Her voice is quiet and firm.

In the morning, they have breakfast on the picnic table outside. The sun is out, but thin. Rose has a dense bruise spreading down her upper arm.

'Is that from yesterday?' asks Graeme.

She smiles. She rests her fingers against it. He can see her press in, the hint of a flinch in the line of her mouth.

She is thin, he thinks, but she is growing. When Caz first brought her round, her pockets were full of food – lint-flecked apple slices, brown and soft, raisins, nuggets of chocolate. They walked in like spiders, her and Aaron, swaying on stick-legs. Wherever she got the food from, it wasn't home.

They play minigolf. Jack wins. They sit on the dunes, then they run down them. Jack chases Aaron. Jack punches Aaron until Graeme tells him to stop. Aaron goads Jack into punching him again and looks at him with hysterical, hopeless adoration.

Rose walks along the line of the surf. Her feet splash through the thin foam. She digs in the shingle for bright stones, vivid and wet, that dry to dull flatness. She watches Aaron and Jack.

They walk together back to the caravan in the mid-afternoon. Rose walks beside Graeme. She's taller than him. As they climb up the path between the dunes she takes his hand.

Graeme lets her. She holds his hand for a minute, then drops it again.

Later, he can still feel her touch. Raw, clumsy. Like affection is a foreign language, badly learnt. He sees it in her face too. Eyes that hold your gaze for a fraction too long, a smile that doesn't quite mean what you think a smile should mean. An unselfconsciousness that has the taint of neglect.

He remembers her mother. Ash. He hasn't seen her for over twenty years, but he still remembers her.

Two hours later, Graeme is woken by Rose screaming.

He fell asleep on the pull-out bed. He stumbles outside. Still light. Rose is screaming at Jack. He's holding both her wrists and laughing.

'Stop!' says Graeme. He pulls Jack away from Rose. Jack releases Rose's hands and she slaps at him, a swinging lunge that just misses.

'Hey!'

Graeme is between them now. He holds his hands up. 'What's going on?'

He feels a dig of pain in his lower back and lurches forward. Rose has pinched him, her nails digging deep.

'Jesus,' he says, twisting and staggering. He sees her, eyes wide and fixed as she lunges past him at Jack.

'Rose!' he shouts, his voice a loud flat bark.

She freezes, swaying. Her arms sink to her sides.

'What on earth is going on?' says Graeme.

Jack laughs.

'Aaron's gone.'

Graeme frowns.

'Where?'

'You lost him!' shouts Rose. Her face is desolate.

The three of them walk up and down the wide beach, shouting. Then they walk along the dunes, shouting down into the sandy hollows and kicking at the tussocks of long grass. The sun is almost gone, leaving a deep blue sky and the pink light of dusk. Rose moves like she is asleep. Her head sways above her long body. Graeme holds her by one thin wrist.

After an hour, Jack finds Aaron in a bunker, concrete, listing in the sand. He sits in one corner, blissfully stoned. Jack calls out, laughing. Graeme lets go of Rose and she runs towards him. She doesn't hug him, but she holds his head in her hands, gently, like it might break, puts her mouth to his ear, and whispers.

Later, Graeme twists in front of the mirror to see the two livid marks that Rose has made on his white back.

When they hit sixteen, Rose enrols at sixth form, and Jack leaves school. He gets a job at the timber yard. Caz tells him he can't stay at Graeme's anymore if he's not in education.

On the last day, Graeme stands at the door. He holds out a hand to shake, but Jack just looks at him. Jack's eyes are black and still, the iris dark and fuller than seems normal. They glisten, as if with the hint of tears, but that can't be right.

They have something in common with the eyes of an animal, Graeme thinks uneasily. Halfway between soulful and soulless.

'Fuck off,' Jack says, with a flash of teeth.

And he's gone.

September.

After school, on the first day of sixth form, Dillon and Alisha walk home together. They talk about their new subjects, about the teachers. About what was boring and what not. They both carefully pretend not to be overwhelmed with the sudden closeness of adulthood.

The conversation drifts off. They walk on. The street is familiar. The stone walls, the concrete paving, the thick yellow paint in fading lines. Only, Oni isn't here. No one has heard from her. She hasn't enrolled at sixth form.

Her absence sits oddly between them. Things will be different without her.

'What do you want to do?' asks Alisha. The air is clean and fresh inside her, and she feels a little scared, a little excited.

They are into Dillon's estate now. Most of the houses are the same. Neat but boxy. Grey, pebble-dashed, three small bedrooms. As you go down towards the river, there's a bigger block, with ten houses terraced together. But they aren't houses, they're flats, each with its own front door, apart from the last door, which is missing. The windows are boarded up, so it looks like a face with eyes closed and mouth open.

Dillon's hands are in his pockets. He feels the cracked face of his phone under his fingertips. He feels his dad's message etched forever under the glass, secret and awful.

'Dillon?'

He says nothing. The square of rough grass at the front of the empty flat is littered with furniture. Six months ago, one of their kitchen chairs broke, so his dad left it there. The chair went from being a part of their home, the chair they all sat on, with a kind of character and life of its own, to being a dead thing. For a moment it looked out of place, rescuable, but by the morning, Dillon could see it was just junk.

'Dillon?'

He blinks.

'What do you want to do, you prick?' Alisha laughs.

He looks away. Refocuses. 'What do you mean?'

'Properly.' Alisha is serious now. 'What do you want to do? Why are you even going to sixth form?'

Dillon shrugs. He smiles uneasily, looks down at his feet.

Alisha frowns as she stares at him.

'Me too,' she says.

In his pocket, against the warm tips of his fingers, Dillon's phone vibrates. He pulls his hand away as if burnt.

On the last day of term, just before Christmas, there is a party at Yannis's house. Everyone says it is a good party. Three emo kids sit on a sofa in the front room the whole night. No one sees them talking. Reece and Ceri have sex in the spare bedroom. It's Reece's first time. His friends wait outside. There is no evidence that they have had sex, but there is also no evidence that they haven't. Ryan gets spiked, and spends the night dancing like a maniac. It's fucking hilarious. Everyone says so.

The best photos that everyone shares afterwards include: several fit girls pouting at the camera; someone's butt;

someone's breast; unexpected people doing gang signs; someone comatose; two people kissing.

At nine thirty Dillon waits in the lit-up front garden, all sharp lines and shadows, neat gravel and round bushes. The sound of the party throbs inside. He has been waiting for five minutes. Eventually he steps forward and knocks. The door opens, letting out warmth, noise, the smile of Xan, Yannis's sister, her legs long and her lips vivid.

He walks in.

The kitchen. A big, wide space, with painted doors and a granite surface. Halls and corridors. A room where people dance – not now, later. Carpets with stains. Strange smells in the bathrooms, potions and vomit. People he knows, transformed. Girls with hair curled, faces smudged. Boys with eyes glazed and hectic. Teeth everywhere.

People are talking. The music is loud, and they talk loud.

'Did you see that thing with the monkey?'

'No.'

'Fucking funny.'

The boys plant their legs wide. They stand like soldiers, self-consciously at ease. The girls look round, to see who's seeing who. They touch shoulders, elbows.

'I love that dress.'

'I love yours!'

Some stand in huddled circles, boys and girls.

'What are you drinking?'

'How much have you had?'

Eyes catch. Jokes fall. Drinks spill. And something sparks, and fires, and they laugh in hysterical wonder.

'Oh my god!'

'That's fucking disgusting!'

'I can't believe that!'

Alisha's looking for Dillon. She has her armour on. She needs to apply makeup in thicker layers these days. Her skin is red and pimpled, with dents and divots where she's squeezed a spot too hard. It doesn't feel like magic anymore, it just feels necessary. She hates the first look in the mirror, but by the end knows it's fine. There's nothing to see anymore.

Last night, in her dream, Oni was there again. It's been six months, but she was as vivid as ever. When Alisha woke, the sense of her friend lingered with the warmth of sleep. She lay still, mouth sticky, eyes closed. When she threw off the covers, the cold air was like growing up.

Once, three years ago, with Oni, she laughed so hard she wet herself. She remembers the giddiness, the heat and pressure at her temples, the swirl of cramp behind her jaw and the deep deep joy that didn't even stop as the hot piss spread through her jeans. She tried to tell Oni, but she just laughed harder, and Oni laughed too, and even when she realised, they lay back on the bed and laughed.

It's not that everything is shit, now. It's that it used to be so good.

When she sees Dillon, he's kissing someone.

Dillon is drunk, and stoned, and as he kisses the girl, her lips are like wet rubber, and he holds and grips at her, and then he stops, because she's so drunk her eyes are rolling in her head. He wonders what her name is. He wonders if he should have just kept going.

She sits down heavily. Her eyelids droop.

'Slag,' says Alisha.

He turns. Grins.

'Who's the new girlfriend, then?'

He blushes. Or would have if his face wasn't so red already.

'I need some air,' he says.

Alisha watches him go then turns back to the kitchen.

In the back garden, smoke curling above the decking lights shimmers and drifts.

The stars are out, and Dillon steps beyond the decking circle onto the freezing mud of the churned-up lawn. The noise of the party is behind him. The cold nips at his neck, at his ankle, and as he draws deep on a joint he feels the old echo of nights on the lawn as a child, when night was strange and scary, glimpsed only on long car journeys and cold Halloweens.

He can see Orion.

He sits on the edge of a low wall, a neat, ornamental boundary running down the side of a path and stretching along the edge of the muddy lawn into the dark distance of the long garden and the bright stars.

'All right?'

Jack's voice is casual as he steps out beside him. Dillon holds out the joint by way of an answer.

Jack takes a deep drag. Passes it back.

'Shit party.'

Dillon shrugs.

'That girl was ugly.'

'What girl?'

'One you were humping.'

'I wasn't humping her.'

'You looked like it.'

'I wasn't humping her.'

Jack grins. 'Maybe you just had an itchy dick.'

Dillon passes the joint. Jack inhales and sits in silence for a moment, letting the smoke out slow. His head sits back on his neck and the angles of it show stark in the light from the house. He seems to be made of a harder substance than Dillon. His bones are closer to the surface.

'I heard about your mum,' he says.

Dillon's fingers brush Jack's as he takes the joint back. Jack's fingers are blunt and fleshy, the nails bitten to nothing. Little nubs of pale pink in a half-moon of angry red tidemarks.

'I'm sorry,' Jack says.

Dillon feels the damp paper against his lips. He holds the smoke as long as he can. He feels dizzy, but it's probably from holding his breath. He lets it out.

'If you need anything.'

That's what people said. It's what they all said. Anything. Anything at all.

Dillon hears his own words as if someone else is saying them.

'You could fuck off.'

He expects at least a punch. He's flinching already. But Jack gets up.

'Sure,' he says.

And he's gone.

Later, after Ryan has been taken home, and Yannis has puked on the stair carpet, and the girl Dillon kissed has collapsed on a sofa with her knickers showing, Dillon wanders through to the front room. It's a different kind of party now, where everything is slicked over with a sticky haze, a slurred filter of strangeness that makes people lean on walls and talk intently in corners.

He sees Jack in the middle of a ring of people. He's staggering, like he's falling. It's funny, and everyone around is laughing big laughs with heads thrown back and stained teeth showing black in the dim light. Rose is there too. She's out of place amongst these heavy bodies, a lanky shadow swaying on thin legs.

Dillon remembers the day in year seven she came to school in bright red heels. They were clumpy and thick at the end of her brittle ankles, cheap and strange and flagrant. She couldn't walk in them. Everyone laughed. She got sent to Mrs Jackson's office.

She places her hands on the back of the sofa, poised for something.

Jack laughs too, thickly, swirling in the crowd. He trips.

Rose steps forward as Jack stumbles. He bumps into her and she steps back again, knocking into someone else. A drink spills on the carpet.

'Fuck's sake.'

Someone pushes Rose.

'Hey!' Jack's voice is heavy, hard.

The room sharpens.

'Easy.'

Jack moves, tense and unconstrained, bucking clumsily. Rose is pushing back at his chest. Everyone's body language is different now. Boys are puffed up, shoulders back, arms wide. Girls are stepping away.

Jack mutters furiously, '. . . fucking touch her . . .'.

His arm sweeps backwards and knocks another glass off the mantelpiece, and someone shrieks and he falls, heavily, and now people are laughing again, louder.

Jack grunts from the floor.

Dillon steps in and hooks an arm under Jack's. He pulls him up. Jack's breath is hot and sweet with alcohol, and the weight of him as he leans forward across Dillon's shoulder is leaden.

The buzz of voices rises and falls.

Dillon's fingers dig into Jack's ribs. They grip tight, like they want to hurt him, but they're holding him. Then someone else is holding him too, and they walk to the door, and they take him out, and they sit him down on the neat step under the bright light at the front door.

Jack, and Dillon, and Rose, and the door is closed behind them.

There is no point at which Rose asks, or Jack asks, or Dillon. They wait outside the door, and nothing happens, and then Jack stands, swaying, and Rose reaches out to one side, and Dillon to the other, and they are walking.

The walk is long and slow, with Jack slung between them. The wet tarmac has a bright sheen under the yellow lights. Jack's heavy steps cause them to veer across the road, and once, to fall.

Jack lives in the grey concrete building above the carpet shop.

They take him in. The hall smells of piss. They help him up the stairs. Three flights. His door has scratches on it, deep, like someone hit it with something.

The door opens. The room is dark.

Before he goes in Jack grabs Dillon's arm above the elbow, tight enough that Dillon almost cries out. Then the door shuts and he's gone.

Rose and Dillon walk back down the stairs. They haven't said a word to each other all evening. Outside the building they stand in the street. Dillon rubs his arms. He realises he's left his jacket at the party.

'It's cold,' he says.

Rose walks over and hugs him.

It's only when someone doesn't do all of the things you expect them to do that you notice the complexity of something like a hug. The arms out, the lean, the smiles, the little noise at the back of the throat.

But with Rose, none of that.

She dives in and holds him tight. His eyes are at the level of her chin, so now her head comes down, bending over him. Her jaw is pressed awkwardly to his cheek. He waits, then he puts his arms around her too, because it seems like the only thing to do.

She rubs his back vigorously. He can feel the sharpness of her body, all bone, surprisingly strong.

'Warmer?' she says.

He laughs uneasily. She disengages.

Dillon wonders if she's drunk. She doesn't seem drunk. He feels like he should kiss her. He's not quite certain what a hug means, otherwise. But he has no idea if she's fit or not.

She's thin – thin like models are thin. But on her it just looks – thin. And her face might be beautiful, if someone else said it was. Or it might just be odd.

'You want to go back to the party?' he says.

She starts to walk. He follows.

'I think I left my jacket,' he says. 'At the party.'

'You think or you know?'

'I know.'

'Oh. You know.'

Her voice is soft, but with a thicker layer of irony in it than he was expecting. He must have heard her speak before, of course.

'Was it a nice jacket?' she asks.

'OK, I guess.' He thinks about this. 'I mean, it was nothing special.'

'What would a special jacket be?'

He shrugs. 'I dunno. Gold buttons?'

'That would certainly be special.'

Is she being funny?

'I know what to look for at Primark now,' he says, testing it out.

Her laugh is a small, private sound. Dillon doesn't know if she's making fun of him. Their footsteps tap along the street to the corner.

'I think I'll go home,' Rose says.

Dillon stops beside her.

'Why?'

She shrugs. She smiles.

When she's gone, he can't help thinking about that smile. It made her face more than just odd, though still not quite beautiful. She looked happy, but also scared. Like happiness was a cliff you might fall off.

. . .

That night, while her students are at their party, and her staff are at the pub, Paula Jackson finally sends a last email and heads home. As she drives, she watches the white line on the dark road. There are not many cars here, on this stretch, at this time. The road curls over the lip of the moors, looping round the town from the squat sixties building that houses her school at one edge to her stone house high on a steep, gardened lane on the other.

The line in the road is bright in her headlights. She imagines crossing it. The car would drift over, the wheels rattling on the cat's eyes. She would drift across, and after one minute, or two, or five, a car or van or lorry would zip over a rise in front of her, and before she had a chance to swerve, she would crumple into it.

She stays steady. She listens to Radio 4. The voices of serious people fill the car. She watches the road. If she went far enough and fast enough, she might sail over the edge, silently, and come to rest gently in the treetops.

Spring approaches. The leaves begin to unfurl. It's something Dillon must have seen before. He must have. But it seems new to him this year how strange it is that they lie curled, whole, inside those buds. He films them on his phone as they flicker in a faint wind, turning as he touches them with a finger, and wonders if he's the first person to do that.

In Media Studies, they are making a magazine cover. Rose sits two desks over, but they don't speak, not in school. As Dillon works, he stares at his screen. He can just catch his own reflection. When he clenches his jaw his face is squarer than it used to be. He thinks it is. It's hard to know.

'Good stuff,' says Mr Bradman.

The teacher leans forward over Dillon's desk. He's a big man, and his presence fills the air around him. He seems young, but he also looks old – his body is thick and muscular, running slightly to fat, and his face is meaty and stubbled and red-cheeked.

He scrolls around in the image Dillon is working on. Dillon follows the cursor as he clicks through the layers of his file, but half an eye is on the big hand moving deftly beside him.

'How old are you, sir?' asks Dillon suddenly.

Mr Bradman gives him a look. His face is somehow nearer to Dillon's than Dillon thought. It's big, like the rest of him. His hair is wispy, light blond and thinning.

'Twenty-six,' he says, his eyes bright with amusement. 'Was that what you expected?'

Dillon shrugs.

Mr Bradman points at the magazine cover.

'Did you take this picture in the same place Rose did?'

Dillon nods.

'It's good. And good to help each other out like that.'

Dillon feels his face redden. Mr Bradman suggests he should let the image overlap the title. Dillon wonders if he should try shaving again.

In April, Mr Bradman announces a visitor. A friend of Mrs Jackson's. A magazine editor.

'This is a fantastic opportunity,' he says. There is something puppyish about him despite his size.

The class don't seem bothered. But Dillon is.

'Will she know about the film industry?'

Mr Bradman shrugs. 'Yes, a bit.'

'What do you mean, a bit?'

'Reviews, fashion, the Oscars – stuff like that. Her magazine covers the BAFTAs. She'll know film people. The media world's a pretty small one. Everyone needs everyone else.'

He talks to Alisha about it later on the bench outside Tesco.

'I'm going into film,' he says.

'Eh?'

'That's what I'm going to do. After school.'

'Like, Hollywood?'

'I don't know. Probably not. But I'm going to make films. I'm going to ask that magazine woman if she'll help.'

Alisha gives Dillon a look of measured approval. 'Fair enough.'

The street is bright and sunny. Anything seems possible.

'Shall we get some weed?' says Alisha.

They text Jack. He's at work. He says he'll meet them at six at the arches. They have an hour to kill. They spend twenty minutes in Poundland, laughing at the own-brand stuff, then throw things off the bridge. The water is strong and fresh. Farther up, the woods are fuzzed and green, with that strong, bright, liquid green of spring.

Along the banks of the river are daffodils.

'Daffodils are shit plants,' says Alisha.

'Seriously?' Dillon plays shocked. 'Daffodils? What's wrong with you?'

She laughs. He throws a can in the water. They watch it bob away.

'Did we ever kiss?' asks Alisha as they walk down under the arch.

Dillon feels dizzy. 'What?'

'Did we kiss? You kissed Oni.'

Dillon tries to laugh. 'No.' He makes it sound like he's disgusted.

Alisha doesn't laugh. 'I just wondered.'

He doesn't look at her, but he can feel her there like an itch. He has no idea why she said that. He has no idea if it means anything. He has no idea if he wants it to mean anything.

He has the familiar sense that he often gets around girls, of being both wildly excited and utterly terrified. There is a kind of lurching thud around his heart. Offbeat.

'All right,' says Jack, coming down the path behind them. Callum is with him. 'All right.'

They're looking at something on Callum's phone. Callum turns the screen round.

'Unbelievable,' he says, grinning.

On the screen is a woman, splayed, someone's arm in her cunt up beyond the wrist.

Dillon looks away.

'Dickhead,' says Alisha.

'You don't like pussy?' says Callum to Dillon.

Dillon says nothing.

Callum chuckles.

'Dickhead,' repeats Alisha.

They buy a bag off Jack. Then they skin up. The four of them share the joint.

When Dillon draws on it, he imagines the slow spread of smoke through his limbs. He exhales smoothly. The wet stone of the arch glints.

'Nice,' he says.

Callum doubles up with laughter. '*Nice*,' he says.

Dillon frowns. He doesn't know what was funny. But Jack is giggling too.

'Nice,' they say to each other, lips pursed, frowning. Dillon smiles, because it's the way of these things. The joint comes round again. He draws deeply. His head fuzzes up.

'Nice,' he says, smiling.

This time Callum's laugh is raucous and loud. He turns to Jack as he laughs, and Dillon can hear the tone of it. Jack splutters, and Callum leans forward, makes a face and says,

'Nice!'

Jack laughs. Callum laughs. Alisha laughs. And then Dillon's head is thick and angry and he says, 'Fuck off.'

Callum steps forward. 'You what?'

Dillon feels his heartbeat thicken in his ears. Alisha looks uninterested.

'Joking,' he says, swallowing his words.

Callum's meaty face breaks open into a wide shout. 'Ha!' Dillon can see his tonsils. Callum points at him, and turns to Jack. 'He's fucking shitting it, this little prick.'

'Leave him alone,' says Jack.

That's the worst thing. Dillon darts forward suddenly and pushes Callum backwards. He falls, and Dillon runs back up the track and round over the bridge, blood racing. He laughs as he runs. Spring can do that to you.

'Have you ever seen an owl?' Dillon asks.

'No.'

'My dad says there's one that lives in here.'

'I've never seen it.'

They sit on the broken stairs, in the dark, in the empty house at the end of the long block. Under their feet is the gritty rubble of the house as it slowly disintegrates. They stopped taking photos weeks ago, but they still meet.

'I finished my essay,' he says.

'Me too,' Rose says.

This is how their conversation goes, mostly. Long gaps, short answers. The slow rhythm of the dark. Silences where his mind starts to wander, and he almost feels like he's talking to himself.

'What do you want?' he asks.

She says nothing.

'Properly,' he adds. 'Not if you could just have anything, but really, things that might really happen.'

He waits.

'You first.'

Dillon narrows his eyes at the inky shadows.

'I'm not sure,' he says. 'Be happy.'

When the words fall, they no longer seem to mean much.

'Make films.'

He pulls his phone from his pocket. He shows her the video of the leaves. The screen floats bright and disembodied against the darkness, the windy day rustling clumsily out of the speaker into the still night.

'I'm going to make a film about the seasons,' he says.

She takes the phone. Her face is lit up by the screen. He watches the reflection in her eyes, and the shade cast in the crook of her nose. A neat scar crosses her temple, straight as a ruler, picked out with a faint shadow in the oblique light.

He grabs the phone back before the clip has finished.

A car moves slowly past on the street outside. As it turns, the headlights touch the inside of the house with a crisp, bright block that sweeps down one wall. For a moment the peeling wallpaper picks out sharp, curled shapes in black down a diamond-patterned wall.

'I want a sofa,' Rose says at last.

He laughs. She doesn't. The car is gone, and in the silent gap it leaves the river churns faintly. He'd never thought of wanting a sofa.

'Why?'

'My mum wanted one.'

'Why?'

'She had these magazines.'

He can hear her mouth. She speaks quietly, and in the night, in the dark, the words are formed against her teeth and her lips. He can hear the touch of them.

'She put pictures of everything she wanted on the wall.'

'But why a sofa?'

'We didn't have one.'

'Why not a house?'

'A house too.'

'Where?'

'Anywhere. Not here.'

Dillon waits.

'The country,' says Rose. She says this like it's a specific place, far away. 'A house in the country. We had a picture.'

They listen to the wind. It blows through the cracks between the boarded windows and their empty frames with a reedy whistle.

'Do you see her?' he asks.

He can feel her silence on his skin, the catch and shift of her breath as she doesn't speak.

'Mine's dead,' he says.

'You told me,' she says.

He can't remember. It seems impossible.

Another car passes. The light slides down the wall. It catches her foot, slim and strange, a disembodied fragment of a person, lying in the debris of the house. Then it's gone.

He wants to stay here, in the dark, in the silence.

'She's in London,' Rose says, eventually.

This is a lie, Dillon knows. It sits between them, delicate and sad.

. . .

Paula walks down her hall, opens the glass inner door, steps onto the carefully restored Victorian tiles, opens the wooden front door. She's changed out of the narrow, tailored skirt suit she wears at school, but her skinny jeans are somehow no less severe.

She greets her sister-in-law, Titch. Titch is a tall woman with a full face. She had been pretty, but her features have thickened with age. In the mornings she looks herself up and down and knows that in the wrong light she is now almost ugly, but she has the right powder and the right lipstick, and just enough mascara to pull it back.

They talk at the dining-room table over wine. They smile at each other, the kind, careful smiles of people practised at smiling, and at the compromises that those smiles are designed to make. They are friends, but friends through circumstance, not choice. It creeps up on you, thinks Titch, and then you realise you've known someone for twenty years.

'I do like your house,' she says. 'You and Andy have such great taste.' Her fingers end in bright acrylic nails that skate delicately over the surface of the table, tapping once or twice. 'I love this table,' she adds.

They sip their wine. The light outside the window dims towards evening.

'I'm a little nervous about tomorrow,' says Titch.

'They're only kids.'

'It's easy for you to say that,' says Titch.

'It's true.'

Titch drinks. She knows Paula is right. She knows that it isn't quite nerves that she's feeling, but that she'd be hard put to find a word for it. The wine glitters in the glass, her fingers resting on the thin stem and touching the underside of the curved bowl.

'I do envy you,' she tries.

Paula raises an eyebrow.

'I do!' she says, laughing. 'It must be so rewarding. Teaching and knowing you're making a difference.'

Paula's face is fixed in light irony. 'No, I'm serious,' says Titch, her hand resting on Paula's. 'You know I am.'

She squeezes the hand under hers, leaning forward, trying to show how serious she is. She smiles warmly at her sister-in-law.

That night, Titch lies in the bed in Paula's spare room. She has the window open, even though the northern air is hard and cold and flutters in though the gap with the wind off the moors. She loves to come here. It feels *far*.

Her mother used to leave the windows open in all weather. She said that condensation was bad for you. She had a brisk certainty about these things.

Next year, Titch will be fifty. She remembers her mother at fifty.

Under her duvet, the heat of her body pools into a pocket of warmth. Her cheeks are cold, but she bundles the duvet high over them. She feels both old and young. She is tired, and so much older than those around her, but she cannot be as old as her mother was at fifty.

In dreams she sees her. They talk, but she has no idea what she is saying.

. . .

Paula has already gone into school by the time Titch gets up. Titch is due to meet her there at eleven. Over breakfast, her fingers skip restlessly across the surface of her phone. Her nervous eyes register the time.

She checks emails, texts. She checks Instagram.

Out of the kitchen window a tall tree threshes in the wind against a blue sky.

She wonders how true it was, what she said, as she gathers her things, as she climbs into the car. Adjusts the mirrors. Rests her hands on the upper curve of the wheel. Words have a way of sticking, once you've said them. She wonders if maybe she really does envy her sister-in-law.

The school is a grey building, square and unappealing. Paula meets Titch at reception. She holds out a hand in greeting.

Titch is slightly put out.

'Thanks for doing this,' Paula says. Serious, then a smile cracks her face. Her cheeks are red. 'It's a little strange, isn't it?'

Titch smiles too and holds Paula's hand in both of hers. 'I've never really pictured you actually *in school*,' she says.

She giggles.

Paula gives another fractional smile, then snaps her gaze towards the door, all business.

They walk through. Paula's in school-tour mode now and she tells Titch about the building, and the number of pupils, and lots of other things Titch has no interest in.

She walks close behind Paula. The kids are in the yard. The sixth-formers wear their own clothes. A boy in a grey hoody looks curiously at Titch as they pass. His face is puffy and nondescript.

'Dillon,' says Paula, stopping the boy. 'This is Ms Parker. She's speaking to your class later about her magazine.'

His pale eyes stare. His mouth opens. He doesn't say anything.

'Nice to meet you, Dillon,' says Titch.

Something has gripped him tight and won't let him move or speak.

'Will you let Mr Bradman know we've arrived, Dillon. He'll be on duty in the other yard.'

Finally, the boy blinks. 'OK,' he says. He gives a tiny, astonished smile as he turns to go.

Something in the line of him, the way he moves off, catches at Titch. Every gesture seems practised, designed for effect, yet so badly done that he walks like someone pretending to walk.

Paula touches Titch on the shoulder, guiding her on towards the sixth form block. At the door, she pauses.

'We refurbished this a few years ago with funds we secured through the local authority.'

Titch isn't really listening. Back across the yard she can see the boy with the grey hoody. He's standing near the other doors. And then, as she watches, another kid, in uniform this time, walks up to him and pushes at his chest. The boy in the hoody swings a fist that hits the other boy with a faint smack.

Titch draws breath in shock.

The movement was so quick and quiet, and now they are thudding into each other, spinning, linked by a hand at the other's shirt and a foot kicking out and caught and then dropped and another blow.

'Fight!' yell voices across the yard, and kids stream towards the two of them.

Paula pivots sharply. She walks straight into the middle of the knot of bodies. Titch's heart is pounding. Kids yell 'Jackson!' and scatter. The two fighting take no notice. They grapple and pull at each other till Titch sees the boy in the grey hoody, red-faced, tumble back towards the door. She sees his elbow strike the reinforced pane and the glass shatters and he falls.

Paula stands in front of the other boy. She's a foot smaller than him. She points and barks something and he goes, instantly, following the line of her finger like it has some occult force. Her lean face is clouded with fury. Her voice is sharp as a whip crack.

The boy in the grey hoody is sobbing on the ground, holding his arm. It looks wrong, the arm. Paula kneels, and he's speaking to her, saying something between choked breaths about having to go to his lesson, he must go to his lesson.

Paula stands, and she shakes her head. Someone takes the sobbing boy in the grey hoody to first aid.

'I am so sorry about that,' says Paula to Titch, as she rejoins her guest, voice tight. They carry on towards the sixth form centre.

Titch's pulse is racing, and the sounds of the school fall spikily around her, sharp and unsettling. The clack of her heels on the floor, the echo of voices. The presence of so many, so close, behind doors, and walls, and windows. She follows Paula as she moves slickly through the corridor, head high and alert, and feels the tightness in her chest of threat, and sudden possibility.

. . .

There are fifteen students in the Media Studies class, spread evenly across five rows of chipped desks. The walls are covered with film posters and student work. Paula smiles at Titch from the corridor and is gone.

The teacher comes to greet her. He is large, athletic in a fleshy and pink-cheeked kind of way.

'Will Bradman,' he says. 'Brilliant you could come.'

Titch hopes she is smiling.

The teacher squeezes himself into a chair at the side.

She tries to meet the students' eyes. She remembers what Paula said last night. They are nice kids, these. These ones are not the ones who fight and smash windows. She sees a skinny boy with a well-shaped quiff, another in a hoody with a couple of pimply chins. A girl with heavy makeup, a dark streak of contouring down each cheek and a white line down the bridge of her nose. Another girl with blotchy hands, stained from fake tan.

Her gaze falls on a tall girl at the back. Her hair falls evenly on either side of her face. Her skin is a little greasy.

The girl meets her eyes. Steady.

Titch blinks first. She widens her eyes, smiles. She takes a breath, tries to slow herself down.

'Good morning,' she says.

As she talks, she feels the tension dissipate. She hears herself talking about the things she knows, and she sees the students' faces looking back at her. She's done this before, in other rooms, with other people. They're not so different here. She speaks about magazines, about the challenges the industry faces. About the daily life of the office. Deadlines, layouts, shoots.

She speaks well, and as she hears herself, she is reminded that, yes, this is what I have achieved, and it is not small. When she finishes, she knows she is smiling, and she knows her face is kind, and that they are listening.

'Have you got any questions?' she asks.

No one moves. She has a moment of sudden doubt. *Were* they listening?

'Come on,' says the teacher. 'They're not normally like this, I promise!'

A small, mousy girl at the front:

'Have you met any celebrities?'

'That's the job. You have to.'

They're impressed. Some of them.

'Who?' asks someone else.

She gives some names.

'How did you get started?'

That from a sullen girl, somehow both sharp faced and full-featured.

'Well,' Titch says. 'I was an intern, and then I managed to persuade them to give me a job as an editorial assistant. From there you've got to work hard – really hard – real dogsbody stuff, you know. Coffee, taxis, all that. And slowly, you gain people's trust – you show them that you're a good fit.'

The girl's face has no expression. 'What's an intern?'

'It's like work experience.'

'How did you get in?'

'That's hard. You have to be really persistent. You have to bug people until they give you what you want.'

'How?'

'How do you bug people? You call them, you write letters, you go in to see them.'

'How do you know who to go to?'

Titch is beginning to find this girl wearing. 'A bit of research,' she says brightly.

The teacher breaks in. 'We can have a little look together, later, Alisha. Other questions?'

'Is everyone like you, miss?'

Titch whitens. The girl asking is the one with the bad contouring.

'Hannah,' says the teacher, his voice even, but with a hint of reprimand.

'I'm not being funny,' she says. She sounds quiet and serious. 'I just mean are there normal people there?'

A boy laughs. Titch feels a cramp in her stomach, a jag of vulnerability.

'You probably think I'm quite posh, don't you,' she says. 'I am, of course.' She can hear her voice in their ears. 'But that doesn't mean everyone is. There's a real range of backgrounds in magazines.'

She pauses. She doesn't know where else to go.

'OK,' says the teacher. 'I think we should wrap it up there. Please do hang back if you have any other questions, but the bell's about to go, so pack up.'

They file out, thanking her. It's nice. They look earnest, and grateful – even the sullen girl, and the one with the contouring. She finds herself agreeing with Paula – nice kids. They do strike her as very different from her interns, though; they seem built according to a different set of instructions.

She tries to think about the current crop. She doesn't

actually know where they went to school. Her editorial assistant sorts it out.

The last student out of the room is the tall girl. She kept her seat as everyone else left. When she does leave, she passes close by. She has the most astonishing eyes, Titch thinks. They are far apart in her face, and have a cool, distant blankness to them. The girl keeps them fixed on Titch until she's walking past, staring her down for just a little too long, with a kind of insolence that's at odds with her mild face. Not rude, though – just a raw interest in looking, without the awareness that someone might look back. When the contact breaks, the girl gives no sign that anything unusual has occurred.

Sometimes feelings can be like scents. You pick them up instantly, viscerally, but you can't always identify them. You can't put a name to them, even as they seem the most vivid callback imaginable to a time you also can't quite name. Titch feels something, an echo, a taint. Something of the longing and pain of being young, something between envy and admiration, between spite and adoration.

The girl is gone.

'Thank you for that,' says the teacher. 'You were brilliant. They got so much out of that.'

The teacher isn't much older than his students, jacket and thinning hair notwithstanding. Eagerness radiates from him. When she was at school she would have mocked him remorselessly.

'I just hope I was of some use,' she says, sounding as awkward as she feels.

He nods. 'Of course, of course... Would you like to see some of their work?'

She hopes the teacher doesn't notice her hesitation. But, 'Yes,' she says. 'That would be great.'

He leads her to the wall. She smiles politely at the badly mounted images, mock double-page spreads for a magazine. Then she looks closer.

The boy is there. The boy in the grey hoody. Standing in a note-perfect scene of urban decay and peeling wallpaper, chin up to show a thin and childish neck, staring straight at the camera. Broken plates litter the ground around him, and his pale eyes are round and serious.

She feels again in her chest that tight, strange sense of threat and possibility.

After the talk, Alisha walks round to the bank of grass at the front of the school. The sun is out. The spring warmth of it is getting stronger by the day. From there, you can see the fells rising above the town. Faint currents of cooler air still curl around the sunny spots, and underneath them, the bank is tinged with damp.

Rose is there, feet up, her coat pulled under her bum.

Alisha's lunch is a Mars Bar and a coffee. She's trying to lose weight. Not really trying, not like the girls who wear gym gear and talk about spinning. But trying. And any other day Dillon would have shared his chips with her.

Rose has a McDonald's on her lap. Alisha sits down next to her.

Rose stiffens slightly, but carries on eating.

Alisha is intrigued at first to see someone so skinny eating so much, but then she turns away. It's hard to put a finger on, but the way Rose looks at her food, the way she holds her chips, even the way she sits, make Alisha uncomfortable.

But she's finished now. She folds her rubbish up and holds it in one bony hand.

'Is Dillon OK?' Rose asks. Her voice is quiet, careful, slow to the point of sounding stupid.

'He's gone to the hospital.' Alisha looks at the folded packet of rubbish and wishes she'd had a Maccy D's. 'He's not dying or anything, but he might have broken his arm.'

'What was it all about?'

'Reece being a prick,' she says. 'Dillon and Callum got into something yesterday, and Reece wanted to act the big man.'

Alisha remembers how she and Oni used to say Rose stank. She did, too. They would spray Rose with Impulse and piss themselves with laughter. Rose never reacted. She wasn't reacting much now, either.

Alisha's eyes narrow. 'Do you like him?' she asks. She thinks she can detect a glow beginning to spread across the girl's pale cheeks.

'Do you like Dillon?' Alisha insists.

Rose's face is still, so still that it seems like an effort of will.

'Do you want me to say something to him?' Alisha asks. There's a gentleness to her tone that even she wasn't expecting.

Rose's fingers move over the little packet of rubbish in her hands, making a faint rustling noise. She shakes her head, but slowly.

Someone calls, 'Rose?'

The lady from the Media Studies talk is there. She's taller than she seemed in the classroom. She's wearing a coat now, a long, elegant coat that hangs down to her well-turned ankles and polished heels. In the classroom, Alisha thought she was weird looking, but now, in the open air, her full, careful face seems younger and kinder. Under the indoor lights you couldn't help noticing how her lipstick didn't quite seem to match the shape of her lips, but here you just saw the red line around her white teeth as she smiled.

'It is Rose, isn't it? I saw your work on the wall. It was just fantastic.'

Her voice is amazing. It sounds like fruit.

'You've got real talent,' she says to Rose. The words stretch at odd places. There's a hiss of saliva behind them. Alisha now wonders if the woman is drunk.

Rose looks up, her neck arcing back, making her body into a snaking loop of bent limbs, from her knees round to her upraised chin. Alisha is struck by how elegant she is. Yet she's also the most ungainly person Alisha's ever met, barring Aaron. Grace and clumsiness seem now to sit side by side in her, comfortably. And Alisha feels herself fade into the background.

No one moves. The ease and polish of Titch hang in the air, even as she seems lost here, caught on a moment's decision. She touches the corner of her eye with her forefinger, then lowers it. The two girls watch her silently.

'Would you like to come for some work experience at the magazine?' she says. 'In London?'

Titch feels a bubble of wonder rise inside her, an expansiveness. She thinks of that sobbing boy and the broken window. Yes, Titch tells herself. Yes, this is possible. Yes, I can be good.

'You could stay with me,' she says. She feels almost weightless. 'You could stay in my house.'

In a wood, beside the train, Rose sees a small lake. A looping, reed-lined shore. An island, with one tree. She's never seen a tree like it. She leans her head against the window, pressing into it as the train zips past. The leaves fall in a curtain, suspended on thin, whip-like branches that trail in the water. The branches curve from the crest of the tree before they hang straight, and it makes the whole thing look like a frozen fountain, green gushing up from the lake and falling back down.

And it's gone.

Tractors, furrowed fields, rising fells and then endless flats. Houses gather, clump, cluster, and then you're in a town, a city, a bridge over a river, a castle rising then falling, and back, fading out into suburbia, and in a flicker, the houses are gone and might never have been.

She keeps her forehead to the glass. It feels good to maintain the contact.

She's eaten her sandwiches already. She has no money for the trolley. It clatters past, the chocolate at eye level. She could just reach out for it.

She wishes Aaron was here.

Her hands rest on the table in front of her. Her sleeves are pushed to her elbows. Her arms are thin, downy with a faint corona of blond hairs. The hollow behind her thumbs is deep.

She looks up to check the strap of her bag as it hangs down. It's a small rucksack. It has a second pair of jeans, five pairs of pants, five pairs of trainer socks, another hoody, a washbag and a notebook in it.

Beside her, a man is eating a huge biscuit.

She touches the back of her hand. She closes her eyes, and imagines her hand is Aaron's.

She opens them. Outside, sheep dot flat pasture. Trees flick past. More sheep.

She rubs her face. She feels her skin move over her cheekbones, her eyeballs under their lids.

She's not worried. It doesn't exactly work like that. She doesn't worry *about* him. His presence in her mind is an instinctive one. Everyone else in the world is on the outside, talking to each other in gestures and words that seem muffled and dim. Aaron is just *there*, in the way her hand is there.

He didn't seem bothered when she left. But she knows him. When he stood at the door, he was crossing his feet, and he was crossing his arms behind his back. He ties himself in knots. His skin is tight on his face, and that seems to squirm in knots too. Crying, for Aaron, is a tool. It doesn't really indicate any particular emotion. But there's a movement in his cheek, under his eye, that looks like something is pulling on the skin of his face from the inside. When she sees that, she knows something hurts.

She should have told him, like she always did. She should have whispered, in his ear, like when they were small and frightened.

Her fingers touch the inside of her elbow. They stroke it, gently.

Back when they lived with their mum, there were no mirrors. She can see herself in the glass, faintly. She is used to not being seen, even by herself.

The evening lowers. The houses cluster. They build. Ten minutes, fifteen, there are just houses going past. They look different. There are more, more warehouses, more railway bridges, more stations, closed and blank as they fly past.

Then a tunnel. Her face appears more solidly against the darkness, hovering behind the surface of the glass. Her temple still touches it, and she sees her eyes, staring obliquely at her from inches away. She winks, one eye then the other.

An announcement. Everyone starts to shift, to stand, to gather things. The sleepy calm of the carriage is gone. Rose stays in her seat. By the time the train is slowing into the platform, most people are standing in the aisle, looming over her. She feels small. The train is cramped. She stays where she is, and her breath starts to catch and she's tempted to stay on the train and wait until eventually it works its way back home.

She watches the platform as they stream from the doors. The stream slows, the carriage is empty, and now Rose rises to her feet. She pulls her bag down. She isn't nervous, not really. The table is scattered with crumbs from the man's biscuit. Absently, she licks a finger and picks them up one by one. Each is a tiny grain of sweetness on her tongue.

She walks forward, because you can always walk forward. She reaches the door, and she doesn't stop. She steps down, and the strange noises, the air, the newness sweep over her. She steps forward.

The pace changes instantly. Another wave of people from the end carriages pours down the long platform, between the trains, under the high roof. They push past her, funnelling her, guiding her towards the barriers, and then she's through them, and into a hall, cavernous, teeming.

She steps forward as the people around her rush past, fanning out across the space. She slows, stops.

'Rose?'

Titch is waiting for her. She has a sign, in case Rose doesn't recognise her. They've met twice now, once at the school gates and once at home, with her foster carer Graeme and Caz, the social worker. But Rose would have recognised her anywhere.

Rose doesn't acknowledge her, though. Her face is frozen. Not that she knows it. Every ounce of her effort goes into looking. At Titch, and at everyone and everything else. The vaulting arches of the station. The crowds. The clothes. The pattern of tiles on the floor.

'Rose?' says Titch again.

Rose marshals herself and dutifully meets the older woman's gaze.

Titch's eyes flicker under the pressure of Rose's stare. She looks away, then back again.

'This way,' she says.

Rose follows Titch down the escalator.

She focuses on the top of Titch's head. Her blonde hair has artful roots. Her neck is tanned, with lines of white in its creases. She wears a top, wide at the neck and long in the arms, that shows a broad, tanned back spotted with moles. She carries a handbag.

Rose wonders if she should have a handbag. She holds tight to the moving black plastic rail.

At the bottom, they walk through tunnels, then go down again. This escalator is longer. The roof arcs above them. Rose looks to the bottom. As they go, they pass dozens of posters, so many they start to repeat themselves. It feels like forever. At the bottom, people step off the escalator neatly, like parcels coming off a conveyor belt, and split into different streams walking down different, narrower, rounder tunnels. Tiled cold walls, clacking feet, and Titch, in front, walking swiftly, handbag in one hand.

Rose takes her other hand.

Titch looks sharply back, shocked, and then whips her face to the front again. Rose lets the hand drop. Titch's feet skitter, a momentary stumble, but she keeps her eyes ahead.

They come to the platform. Now Titch turns, and smiles. 'Here we go. This is my line.'

A gush of warm air roars down the tunnel. Rose grabs for Titch's hand. This time she holds on tight as the train roars in. Her panic subsides as it slows and stops, slick and tidy and without fuss. The doors slide, and they step on, and she's still holding Titch's hand even though she's OK now, because neither of them knows how to let go. They stand around the pole in the centre, and Titch's face is pale, and scared, and Rose doesn't know why Titch would be scared but feels a swell of pride that, now, she isn't. She drops Titch's hand.

The train moves smoothly off.

. . .

Titch's flat is in Chiswick. You say 'Chizzick'. The Underground is the Tube. By the time they arrive they've managed to find seats, and the Tube is no longer even underground. Rose steps lightly, buoyed up by excitement. The station they get off at is small, like a pretend station. It's almost dark, but the sky still has a blue glow to it. The streetlamps are on. The air is warm, the street is clean and bright.

They walk to Titch's flat, in an ornate block, with red bricks and white bricks and a huge window over the door. There are neat, cropped gardens outside, narrow hedges the height of a cat. The bells at the entrance are brass, shiny, with typed name tags. In the hall, the tiles loop and branch across the floor in curled geometric patterns. At the bottom of the staircase you can see up, and above the hard flights of straight stone steps the bannister twists towards the skylight in a flattened spiral.

Titch takes her post from a wire cage by the door. They climb the stairs. Rose runs her fingers along the wooden rail. The nicest house she's been to is Yannis's, at his party, but it's different when people are vomiting. She doesn't know what to expect. Graeme's house is nice too. The first time she was there she thought it was the cleanest place she'd ever seen. It had a sofa and two armchairs that lift up when you pull a lever. It had a kitchen with shining surfaces, and a picture of cows on the wall. To imagine some place even better would have been to enter the realm of pure fantasy. She knows that there are palaces in the world, and houses with swimming pools, and people with servants, but the idea that one might actually go to a place like that, or meet the people who live there, seems ridiculous.

But not so ridiculous now.

Titch opens the door. A long corridor stretches before them. Rose steps forward with a sense, not of shock, but of liquid strangeness.

The corridor is grand. The ceilings are high. At the far end is a mirror, and in front of the mirror, a sculpture. But on hooks on one side are coats, piled high and beneath are shoes, stacked on a shelf. There are pictures on the walls. Too many pictures. The floor is wood, inlaid in little diagonal tiles, with a long, shabby, patterned rug on top.

She steps forward. The air is dusty and perfumed. The flat is small.

'Sorry it's such a tip,' says Titch.

The pictures are not pictures as Rose knows them. One has a few lines on a textured piece of paper. Another shows a man standing on a globe, a fierce expression of grief and horror on his face, while he tears with his teeth at a severed human leg, and crowds of goggle-eyed figures stare from the edges.

'Good, isn't it?' says Titch, brightly. 'It's an eighteenth-century political cartoon.'

Rose stares at the carefully rendered tendrils of meat that hang from the man's teeth.

'Come on in,' Titch says.

They step into a room.

'This is the drawing room,' she says.

Rose stares. It looks like a living room.

'And this is the loo,' says Titch, opening a door.

Rose obligingly peers into a small toilet.

'Kitchen – help yourself to anything – and dining room.'

Rose leans over Titch to look. A fitted kitchen is clogged with bottles and jars on every surface. None of it looks like food.

'And your room. You've got an en suite.' She smiles. 'You must be tired. I'll leave you to it.'

When the door closes behind Titch, Rose sits on the bed, then lies back, and looks up at the ceiling.

She stands, goes to the toilet attached to her room. She wonders what the *en suite* is.

Sitting on the toilet, she looks around. It's like a normal room in miniature. It has books in it. She picks one up. It has cartoons. She reads one. It's about people and horses. There seems no particular point to it. There are pictures on the wall. One is a pen and ink drawing of a house with a thatched roof and roses climbing the walls. It looks like Grandma's cottage in 'Little Red Riding Hood'. She wipes herself, still staring. A curl of inky smoke swirls from the chimney.

Rose doesn't normally dream. But here she does. She dreams of clean sheets, and then she wakes in them, damp, and she drifts off again. The air is dense, warm. She dreams of Aaron, beside her in the bed. He rolls and stirs, restless, and she wakes and his legs are her legs, and she sleeps. She dreams of a long corridor, and a tatty rug, and windows through which flick scenes – a lake, a house, a man chewing on a leg. The sheets bunch around her and she knows she's hidden what she needs in them somewhere. She rolls and twists, and in the sheets is the place where she's hidden the trolley, the rack of chocolate, the bags of crisps.

She comes to with the smack of waking after a fever, the wide, drenched suddenness of it. The sheets are wet, and the mattress is exposed. She can feel the imprint of a button in the small of her back.

At breakfast, Titch has muesli and yoghurt, while Rose has toast and jam. Rose has orange juice. Titch has coffee.

Rose watches Titch eat. She puts the spoon in her mouth delicately, with a small, neat amount of yoghurt and a practised curl of the handle to make sure nothing is sloppy or spilt. She has the yoghurt first, then coffee. When she sips it, her eyes slip up over the top of her cup. Rose meets the glance, and Titch looks down.

Rose remembers the feel of her hand.

Above the table is a photo, of a cottage like the picture in the bathroom. Not just 'like', but almost identical, down to the roses, the thatch, and the curl of smoke. Rose can see the clean bright white of the walls, the black of the half-timbered frames around the door and the windows. It's disorientating – as though something she imagined has been made real. She's never seen anything so pretty.

Rose asks, 'Is that the house from the toilet?'

Titch smiles. 'Yes. I did a pen and ink from the photo. Not very good so I hid it away.'

'Is it real?'

Titch is startled. 'What do you mean?'

'Is it a real place?'

Titch smiles. 'That's my other house.' She hesitates. 'In the country.'

Rose stares at her. 'Really?'

Titch smiles again, a different smile this time, wide and helpless and unable to conceal her pleasure in Rose's innocence. 'Yes.'

Titch gives Rose a key, and makes sure her phone is charged. They will head in together, but Titch says she may have to stay late. She gives Rose a little folded paper map of the Tube, with their stop circled in blue pen.

'It's straight down on Piccadilly,' she says.

It's much better this way round. Starting at a small station above ground and then getting out at Covent Garden, still deep underground, but always rising. Escaping rather than descending.

They step out of the station into bright sunshine. The street is busy. Busier even than the train. Not busy like the high street at home, but busy like the outside of a football ground, or a corridor in school on lesson changeover. Busy so you can't cross the flow of people, who move fast, in bright, summery dresses, in light jackets and shorts, in sunglasses. All beautiful, all young.

They cross, and walk up towards Titch's building.

Rose moves slowly, her head tilted up. The buildings are tall, the roads narrow. The shops are bright, glossy. Like the inside of a shopping centre, but outside. Not like a high street at home, with charity shops and newsagents, and Burger King and Marks & Spencer. The windows have sparse, elegant displays. A coffee shop has a queue out into the road.

Titch's building has glass doors. A man and a woman behind a desk, then the lift. It's not quite as impressive as Rose had hoped. She thought it might look more like one of the shops.

But Titch smiles at the people behind the desk, and they smile, and say, 'Morning,' and they walk up and Titch says, 'This is Rose.' And Rose wakes up.

They look at her. She blushes. She'd felt invisible, but now the thought that people will meet her and ask her name and she will have to talk to them changes everything.

'Rose will be here for the next four days on work experience.'

She swallows, and the movement flutters on through her gut. In her stomach, a familiar, burning hunger stirs.

'We'll need to get her a pass.'

They smile. They nod. They give her a pass. She clips it to the neck of her T-shirt. With the pass she only feels more exposed. She's wearing jeans, a T-shirt, trainers. Titch said the office wasn't formal, but this place is formal. Titch is wearing a dress and heels. Rose feels too young.

Her arms cross in front of her stomach. Her long fingers touch the skin of her wrists. In the lift, she sees herself in the mirrored walls. She leans close to Titch.

'I don't think I'm dressed right,' she says.

Something in her tone makes Titch look at Rose properly for the first time that day. She doesn't look away or look down. The faintest touch of triumph creeps into her expression as she says,

'You're fine.'

After a slight pause, she adds, 'You're beautiful.'

With her face made up and her hair perfect, Titch is like someone from the telly. She looks like someone Rose's mother would have wanted to be.

'So are you,' says Rose.

She can see the flush rise up Titch's neck. Her eyes keep steady on Rose, though. At most they crinkle at the corners. Then her hand moves quickly, grasps Rose's, and squeezes it.

'You'll be great.'

The lift doors open. The office is a wide, open-plan space. It doesn't look that special, but the figures who move between the desks walk with confidence, and are dressed in a uniform of effortless cool. Most are women, but the few men aren't like men Rose knows. They look like they've been assembled with care, with bright shirts buttoned at the top collar, ironic jackets and glasses with thick square rims.

Rose takes it in with two simultaneous narratives running in her head. Part of her sees something surprisingly ordinary next to the exoticness of the rest of London, while another part sees these people move with a kind of phosphorescence trailing in their wake, an enchantment borne of knowing exactly who and where they are, and having no doubt that they belong there.

Titch stops as she enters the room and Rose bumps into her. She turns, smiles, walks on, up to a girl at a computer at the edge of the room.

'Rachael.'

The girl is white-skinned, with dark hair, almost black, and it falls in thick silky sheets around her face. She is pretty. She has the things pretty girls have – the eyelashes, the lips. Her skin is smoothed with well-applied foundation. But when she gives them her attention, and when the hair falls differently round her face, Rose sees that Rachael's jaw is heavy, and her neck thick, and when she turns a certain way her nose looks funny.

But she is pretty. She dresses like she's pretty, and her eyes sparkle like she's pretty as Titch makes the introductions.

'Rose is seventeen,' Titch is saying, 'and she's very talented, and she's staying with me. So look after her.'

And then Titch is gone. Gone through a door at the far end of the room.

'Don't look so scared,' says Rachael. 'You'll be fine!'

Rachael's voice is strange. Titch sounds like the queen, or at least how Rose thinks the queen would sound. Old and posh. Rachael is posh but different. She speaks quickly, with words that run into each other, then crash dramatically into one syllable, drawn out theatrically at the end. You'll-be-*fiiine.*

'How do you know Titch?' she asks.

It takes Rose a while to figure out what to say. By the time she's got her words lined up, Rachael's speaking again.

'You've totally played a blinder, by the way. She never does favours. Are you related?'

Rose shakes her head.

'Where do you live normally?'

'I'm not from London,' Rose says.

Rachael's eyes widen. 'Oh my gosh. Say that again.'

'I'm not from London,' says Rose obediently.

Rachael's face lights up. 'I love it!' she says, clapping her hands. '*Loon dun.* I love it!' She leans forward. 'I absolutely love it. I love northern accents.'

The hairs stand up at the back of Rose's neck. Once, she'd been walking alone down the high street, walking home from school, and she passed a man on one of the side streets. She didn't look at him as she passed, but when she got to the corner by her turn-off two hundred yards on, she turned. He was still there, his eyes still on her. All the rest of the way home, although he had gone, she felt that the rules had changed, and she was being watched.

She feels the same now.

Over the course of the day, Rose makes some tea, looks over Rachael's shoulder a lot, and organises a box of stuff. The box of stuff is in a cupboard. Rachael calls it the 'crap pile'. She says people just give them stuff.

Rose sits in the cupboard sifting slowly through the box. It's filled with fitness DVDs, celebrity biographies, chick lit, and face cream. There's a headband with two balls on springs, one with a picture of Prince William and the other with Princess Kate. There's a pair of knuckledusters.

Each item she examines carefully. They are new, but given away. The idea of it seems miraculous. She puts a lip gloss in her pocket.

After a while, she gives up on the box and leans back against the wall. Above her are rows of dresses, hung messily on a rail. Various odd shoes litter the floor.

Rose takes her phone out. She hasn't looked at it since coming to the office. It's an old phone, something Graeme found and gave her a couple of years ago. When she left for London he gave her strict instructions not to let the battery run down, so she's kept it turned off until now.

Three new messages. One from Graeme, saying

All OK?

Another from Aaron saying

good night

And one from a new number

Hi Rose, Its Dillon, I got your number from aaron hows it going?

In the dark of the cupboard she feels the swirl of surprise blooming along the alleys of her body until it tingles at the edges of her.

At six, the office heaves in a collective sigh. Most people rise from their desks. Some stay, finishing things, but the bulk of them head to the lifts, talking, laughing.

Rose doesn't leave with the others. She's avoided saying any words as much as she could, today. She ate her lunch on her own in the cupboard. It wasn't bad. It was nice, sitting there, unseen.

When there are only a few people left, Rose goes to Titch's door. She knocks.

Titch shouts, 'Come in!'

The office is nothing special. She expected it to be more. But it's just another desk with a computer Titch is staring into. With glasses on. Rose hasn't seen her in glasses before. Titch takes them off when she sees Rose.

'Good day?' she says, brightly.

Rose nods.

'I have to stay late, I'm afraid. If you head back, I'll be there by nine.'

Rose doesn't move.

'Maybe you could look in a few of the shops round Covent Garden before taking the Tube.' Her smile fades a little. 'You're OK on the Tube, aren't you?'

Rose nods. She smiles hesitantly. 'Bye,' she says, then turns to go.

The street outside is busier even than in the morning. It's Tuesday, but people are sitting outside cafés and pubs and restaurants. The day is still sunny, and the warmth sits comfortably on the street, filling all corners. At home the lick of wind is never far away, and every shadow hides a cool shiver.

I *am* OK, Rose thinks.

She's been places on her own before. More than most. But sometimes, sitting with Graeme, and Mrs Jackson, and Caz, it's also seemed like she's weaker than most. When they speak, they talk over her. She doesn't say anything. When they met to discuss her coming to London, she barely spoke three words.

'If she was my daughter, I'd absolutely let her do this.'

'But she's not, Graeme.'

They said things. Rose listened. Sometimes they asked her questions and she shrugged, nodded. Shook her head.

'I'll be OK,' she said.

She walks down the street towards the Tube station. She has an Oyster card for the Tube, but she also has some money. Fifty pounds. Titch is giving her breakfast and dinner for the four nights she's here, and letting her make sandwiches for her lunch. She doesn't know what the fifty pounds is for.

She walks slowly past the shops, drawing the time out before she has to get on the Underground. She looks at the clothes in the windows. The displays are like the adverts in *Vogue* that she used to leaf through, filled with mannequins who wear clothes that fall just right over their limbs, that drape and slide and swoosh and *fit*. She never would have thought real people could be like that, but the streets here are full of them.

But not everyone. She spots people like her too. People in jeans and T-shirts, people who are a bit too fat, or whose knees bend inwards, or who walk like they're apologising.

A deep, rich scent of coffee wafts past. A laugh, a blast of perfume.

Rose knows she's not too fat. She knows her knees don't bend inwards. But she also knows that when people get close to her, they recoil. She knows that she doesn't have what all of these people have, what even the mannequins have – that cast-iron grasp of how to hold yourself in relation to others. Nodding heads, holding hands, even something as simple as looking. The only person Rose infallibly knows what to do with is Aaron.

Another window. There are trainers here. Hundreds of them, artfully arranged. She's been to JD Sports, but she knows this is different because of the clear white space between things. She lets her face sink towards the glass, feels the cool touch on her forehead. She's wearing running shoes. They're old. She could get new ones. But she knows these will not be fifty quid.

She walks on. She crosses the road in front of the Tube station. The entrance to it is thronged with people. So busy that she can't get close. She watches them press through the turnstiles, and thinks of the tunnels inside, the lifts heading down, the passages sighing with warm air.

She walks past.

The street is pedestrian now. People painted silver stand on boxes. She doesn't know why. The street opens out into a square, with a building in the middle lined with pillars. Tables from cafés spill out, and people circle, drifting. She walks, because when she stands still people bump into her. Round a corner, she finds a low step beneath another row of pillars, and she sits.

The sunlight paints a vivid stripe across the buildings opposite, but where she sits is in shadow. It's not cold, though.

The stone is warm underneath her, and the air is warm. She feels sticky in her jeans.

She takes her phone out.

Hi Rose, Its Dillon, I got your number from aaron hows it going?

She types, slowly.

Its good

A group of people walk past following someone holding up a little yellow flag. A small boy walks in from the other direction, holding on to his mother with one hand and clasping an ice cream in the other. He gazes blankly back at Rose as he licks his dripping cone. Chocolate on his nose, eyes wide, wet and still with the intensity of his pleasure.

Maybe she should buy an ice cream with her money.

But now Rachael is there. 'Rose!' she calls, delighted. Her face is bright, her smile gleaming. 'How are you! What are you doing?'

Rose is determined not to speak. Rachael's voice drops into a tone of deep concern. Unless she's just taking the piss. Rose can't tell. 'Are you OK?' she asks.

But she can't help it. Rose can't stop a smile spreading across her face, and she blushes and says, 'I'm fine,' and she smiles again, because suddenly, she feels warm and happy, and the astonishment of it takes her breath away.

Rachael laughs. 'I thought something had happened!'

Rose can't stop smiling. She hugs herself.

'I'm going for a coffee,' says Rachael. 'Do you want to come?'

Rachael: tall, pretty, adult. Behind her the white stone buildings gleam.

'Yes,' Rose says.

. . .

Rachael knows all the words, and how to use them. When she orders her coffee, she does it in a way that implies an absolute certainty that she will be listened to. Her voice is loud. It's quiet too, when she wants. She seems to go through a greater range of expression than anyone Rose has ever met. Her gestures match. Her hands move, and her arms move. When she laughs, she leans forward and her head bucks back elegantly or dips down shaking.

Rose sips her drink. It's a chai latte. She's never bought one before. At home she makes tea, sometimes, but she doesn't know why you would buy one of these when you could buy a cake or a fizzy drink. Or an ice cream.

Rachael talks. About Titch, and work, and clothes. She asks Rose questions, but most of the questions come with their own answers.

'Don't you just love a chai latte?'

Rose nods.

After the café, they go to the shops. Rose wouldn't have gone in on her own. The doors are high, the glass sparkles. But Rachael marches her in.

Rachael tries on clothes. She goes into the changing room and comes out with clothes that look great, or less great, and then she buys them. Rose tries nothing on. She just watches.

Rachael moves through this world like she owns it. She takes things that she wants, off racks and shelves, messily, carelessly, and buys them. Not things that she needs, like food, but things that she wants, for no reason other than that she wants them. Rose tries to imagine what that would be like.

. . .

That night, Rose dreams again. Her dreams are busy. People stream in and out, in bright wisps of wonder. She wakes, sweating, exhausted by the buzzing of her head. She drifts through conversations and escalators. She dreams of Rachael's teeth, white and even. She dreams of food, plates and plates of food, cakes piled high and hot chocolate in a mug the size of her head. She dreams of Rachael biting down on her own arm.

In the morning, they eat breakfast. Rose's fingers move on the edge of the table, tapping restlessly. Thin fingers, with small white nails marooned at the end. She used to bite her nails, years back. When she first went to Graeme's, she bit her nails, but she stopped. She clips them whenever she can to stop herself from biting them.

Titch has long nails. Her hands, smooth, slightly swollen, end in clean, bright colour. Her fingers move with elaborate care to keep the click of the nails from interfering with their movement. On her phone they tap faintly.

'Rachael said I could go to a premiere tonight,' Rose says.

She nurses the excitement like a flame inside her. She remembers Rachael, her voice casual, but her face alert with curiosity. She remembers the moment they parted. Rachael gave her a hug. Rose had no idea it was going to happen. She stood there, shocked, while Rachael and Rachael's perfume enveloped her. She could smell it for hours.

That smell was the smell of wonder, now. She held it in her nostrils as she thought of a premiere. A red carpet. Film stars. Swimming pools. Ice cream.

Titch barely registers this. 'Sure,' she says. 'That would be a lovely idea. She'll go too, will she?'

Rose nodded.

'Why don't you take something from the office to wear? There must be something in the cupboard.'

There are three of them. Rachael, Jacqui from the reviews desk, and Rose.

The amazing thing about the crap pile is the way that when stuff is put there, it becomes crap. In a box, in a cupboard, a strappy sandal looks tacky and slight, a confection of tinsel and cardboard. Loose, it happens almost at once, but even wrapped, in packaging, in cellophane, a dullness falls. A dress comes in, new, is passed around, admired, then put away, and when you go to look again the sheen is gone. A faint film of dust dimming the sequins, a crease, the haphazard fall of clothes off the hanger. Then Rachael picks it, shakes it, holds it against Rose, and Jacqui from reviews nods, and Rose blushes, and she looks at the size of it and knows she can't wear something like that but they squeal, and they shriek, and her face is hot, and she has to speak, even though she doesn't like to.

'I can't,' she says.

They won't take no for an answer.

'You're so skinny! It'll be *perfect*.'

They tell her to change.

'Where?'

Here. They giggle. They look at her. And Rose knows nothing. She knows nothing about them. They are old, and they are adult, and they know the rules.

She wants to take it to the toilet. They tell her to change here.

'Where?' she asks again.

'Here.' In the cupboard. In the crap pile.

She undoes her buttons. Pulls down her jeans. Pulls off her T-shirt. Pulls the dress quickly over her.

In the space between, when she stood in her underwear, hunched over herself, she felt their silence. A prick of it, a stipple against her skin, the little pointed glances they made.

It is still there, now, on the tarmac, at the frayed edge of the red carpet.

There are velvet ropes either side, and people crowded behind them. There are photographers, and Rose can see people in fancy dresses and suits standing while the flashes go off.

But it's also a carpet on the street. She can see grubby marks on the paving stones underneath it.

She looks up to where the flashes are. Whoever it is must be famous enough for a photo. But they're also tiny and far away.

She feels the familiar doubleness that has stalked her trip to London. This is a fantasy, a fairy tale, but it's also utterly ordinary. Sometimes she feels older than she is, older than she possibly could be.

Rose looks down at her legs, long, bare, white. The fringe of the dress hangs mid-thigh. She doesn't know how to walk in this, so she walks like she always does, long stepped, dreaming. The sandals they picked for her look different on feet. The gold is now gold, the straps elegant and curved over her ankle.

They fit perfectly.

Rachael and Jacqui clack hard heels in small steps beside her.

She feels the air on her, the warm London air. She watches the people as they get closer, and the flap of her sandals muffles as they step onto the carpet. Her eyes are strange. They put mascara on her. She feels the heat of bronzer on her cheeks. She feels small inside herself.

People are looking.

Rachael and Jacqui notice it. They notice that Rose doesn't. She fills the same space she did before, an awkward, thin, adolescent space, childlike, boyish, half ugly, ready to be kicked a bit, prodded a bit, poked at and laughed at for not being *there*, not being *right*, not knowing who she is or how to use it. Only that space, framed here, in that dress, on this carpet, looks different.

It's a very strange magic. A turn in perception. The person that you know up close becomes another in a new context. And all those tics, the little oddities, the alien quality of her, become a mesmerising charisma. Rachael is staring too. Half laughing. She can't tell if she's witnessing the birth of a star or the moment the curtain is tugged aside by a small dog and all those supermodels are revealed to be shy, damaged teenagers, with a come-hither gaze that, on closer inspection, is a look of pure fear.

And the flash. The burst of it. A crackle, faint and distant. In the pack of black-suited men, one of them is sharp and present as she turns, as the dress flares, as his eyes glint behind a lens, curious.

Jack turns the pages of the magazine as he waits. As he often does, he sits with one hand down the front of his tracksuit bottoms. There is no one there apart from the receptionist. He wouldn't actually wank at the GP's, but he's still half hard.

He's reading *Vogue*. Not reading. Looking. Page after page they stand, lips parted, eyes drowsy, willing him to fuck them with their elegant dresses and shiny skin. They are polished, glistening with the sheen of a million eyes. Shoulders drop, hips jut, feet point in delicate arches. Little slivers of flesh, the narrow band between a thigh and the line of a swimsuit, the cut of a skirt high over a hip, the deep vent that billows open to the navel, covering fortuitously both flat, perfect breasts.

A sharp beep sounds. *Mr Jack Fenwick Room 4.*

He stands. Draws his hand from his waistband. Walks through. Rolls his shoulders as he walks, maybe more than normal. The corridor is narrow, and clean, and the smell of doctors seeps along it.

He opens the door to Room 4. Dr Flint is there. He knows Dr Flint.

'Jack,' says Dr Flint. 'Sit down.'

He sits. He starts to roll up his sleeve.

'How are you feeling?'

'Fine.'

He can feel the sweat under his arms.

Blood pressure first. Then Dr Flint asks him to look up and to one side. He peers in with a bright light, his face inches away. His skin smells bland, soaped and cleaned. Almost close enough to feel the warmth. Stubble deep-set and blue, and the faint moist heat of breath, held in politely, but seeping shallowly from his nostrils as he concentrates.

And away. Distance is restored. Needles next.

'We'll do all the tests today. Your eyes aren't great. Have you been looking after yourself?'

Jack shrugs. The touch of the needle. The sharp surprise as it slides in. He looks away while the blood fills the vial. He's been doing this for years now. He used to accept it as just part of life, but he finds himself increasingly bothered. He is alive now, adult in a way he wasn't even three months before. When he walks to work in the morning, he notices things. He doesn't know why, but he hears sounds in a sharper way. Tyres on the street, a conversation behind him, the rustle of leaves. He doesn't listen to headphones when he walks anymore. He finds himself rarely less than high, and not because he's been taking something. It's like a switch has been flicked.

And the blood bothers him.

The thought of it itches. He rolls his sleeve down again, but he can feel the pinprick where he has been breached, and where they will carry on breaching him. Inside is the other, the sickness, sprung from somewhere unspeakable.

'OK?' asks Dr Flint.

'Yeah.'

He pulls his jacket on.

'We'll let you know.'

As he walks back down the corridor, he feels his swagger returning. Fuck this, he thinks. He feels the words in his mouth. Fuck this. His lips move. The kick and hiss, the click on his palate, soothes him. He can see the flowers at the front of the clinic, the bright sun against the dirty glass doors, and he barrels out, half skipping, just as Dillon steps up.

'Hey.'

The sound is reflexive, cautious. Dillon acknowledges him warily.

Jack smiles. He uses his teeth. 'You all right, bud?'

Dillon nods. Jack swings round, his feet moving restlessly. He looks like he wants to run. Like he might sing or hit someone.

'I'm late,' says Dillon. He isn't.

Jack grins wider. And for no clear reason he hangs his mouth wide, wolfish, then snaps his teeth together with a clack. He throws his head back and laughs, and dances down the path.

In the waiting room, Dillon picks up *Closer*. He skims the pages. He sees bad flesh circled, pants showing. He looks closely to see how much you can really make out in the poorly printed grain of it. He flexes his left hand. The faint ache deep in his bone is still there, but this should be the last check-up.

He wonders where Rose is.

Aaron is fourteen now. He is tall, thin, and his awkwardness is hardening into something sharp and strange. He often misses school. When he does, he goes down to the river, up the path into the woods. He walks for hours. Sometimes he goes up on the fells.

He wears a hoody under his blazer. He wears trainers, and his coat is old and worn. On the fell tops, in the heather, he holds it round him with his hands in his pockets. It looks like it could pass round his body twice. There is a limestone rock he goes to, cresting through the purple flowers like a breaking wave. He sits on it in the sun, under it if the wind cuts harder. There is a crack in it where he keeps a pack of cigarettes. In the fresh wide air the smoke whips thinly up. Walking the paths, you might catch the tail of it.

In school, he sits at the front. His teachers think this will make him learn better. He stares at what they write. He copies it down. His writing spiders across the page. His fingers don't seem to trust pens. He can't hold a margin. If he writes a paragraph it slopes down the page as if the words are leaking away.

They tell him things, and he does what they say. Someone works with him. She sits beside him in English, and they read *Macbeth* together. He understands it. He has been told the story, and when the teacher explains what it's about, he gets it. But when he looks at the words in the book, he gets nothing.

Macbeth is the worst, but it happens with the others too. He reads a poem. He listens to what the teacher says. She says the word 'rustled' is onomatopoeia. He writes it down. She says isn't it sad? He writes down that it is sad.

All knowledge is equally far from him. He does his duty, but he has no idea why Wordsworth is writing about going out in a boat. That's not true: he knows why, because the teacher has told him, but the idea that the poem should speak to him is as absurd as asking why it is he likes the fells, or why it is Jack makes him feel loved. Poems exist, and the fells exist, and Jack exists, and Aaron walks between them with a splinter of ice deep in his heart.

The day after the premiere, Rose wakes late. The day hits her with a smack of light, a quick surfacing from the depths. Her face is warm, and she feels the stickiness of sleep in her mouth and in the crook of her elbow.

Her dress is on the chair. It hangs, tiny, a scrap, like nothing. She remembers the feel of wearing it. The strangeness of not being herself.

She swings herself from the bed. She stands. She looks at her legs below the T-shirt she wears in bed. She sees the bend of them, above the knee, the bow, the thin thighs. She rests her hands on them. Her fingers touch a few inches above the knee.

She pulls on jeans.

Rachael smiles as Rose walks into the office. A new smile. Her face moves forward as she does so, reaching out, teeth first. Her eyes are hungry.

'Oh my god. That was incredible!'

Rose can't stop her mouth cracking open into a matching smile. She sits behind it, curious, her face mirroring Rachael's.

'What was his name?'

Rose remembers the heat of his breath on her.

'Jacqui!'

Jacqui is here now.

'Was he fit?' asks Rachael.

Jacqui nods. 'Yeah.'

Rose tries to picture him. Dark hair. Loose and curly. She can feel it on her neck.

'Did you get his number?'

Rose shakes her head.

'What was his name? You can message him.'

She tries. She thinks back through the maze of the evening. The feel of her feet on the carpet. The air, cool under the hem of her dress. In the lobby of the cinema. People standing around waiting. They aren't the important people. The celebrities go somewhere else. But these people wait and they look like they might be important, or at least that they're used to importance, accustomed to it enough that this lobby, this carpet, none of it matters.

They sit at a table. Rose, Jacqui, Rachael. He comes over. He speaks. They stand. She can feel the story surround her. He is handsome. He holds a hand to her arm.

He is handsome.

'You don't know his name?'

Rose raises her eyebrows apologetically.

'Oh my god.' Jacqui turns to Rachael. 'She doesn't know his name.'

'I can't believe you don't know his name.'

Rachael's eyes shine bright.

'Does he know your name?'

Rose shakes her head.

'But he kissed you!'

He kissed her. Lips, the wet strangeness of a tongue. Rasp of stubble. A hand at the small of her back.

'Oh my god,' says Jacqui. 'Don't worry!'

'I'm not worried,' says Rose. Her voice is firm. 'I don't care.'

They don't reply. They watch her as she walks off to the cupboard. Her legs move slowly, her head remains still. Her shoulders are thin.

On the train home, Rose curls up in her chair, her knees by her chin, her arms wrapped round them. Her eyes rest on the fields, on the cars, the houses. On the tick of the pylons, the clouds in slow pyramids, the swirling birds.

She remembers him.

He comes to the table. She stands with him. He is shorter than her. Rachael and Jacqui stand too. They talk. He asks things. She says nothing. Not one word. His hand rests on her arm, the slightest touch, but it rests there, like any moment he might grab her tight and usher her away somewhere.

They go in to watch the film.

In the dark she feels his fingers. He isn't there, but his fingers are. They press, ghostlike, into her skin all through the film, and at the end, when the lights are on, and they walk out, he's there again. He walks over to them. He is alone. In the evening, Leicester Square is bright, and the London night sits waiting. She is to go home, soon, not yet, but soon, and he takes them to a bar, and she goes, and no one asks how old she is, because tonight she is someone new. London Rose. Rose in a dress. Rose with the hot marks of fingers at the back of her elbow.

He buys drinks. She asks for coke. She gets rum and coke. She drinks it, at a table, and the sweetness of it seeps into her. And she starts to talk.

She doesn't know what she says, but she feels her words tumbling out, pebble smooth and northern, and she hears him hearing her, and her difference, and her age, and the others go somewhere, and they return, and he has been speaking to Rose, just Rose.

The bar is full. Words rattle and hang, fast and warm and sweet with wine and coke. The lights are sharp and dazed, the people tall and slick, the room full, with arms and shoulders and damp tabletops sticky with someone else's spillings.

On the train, the window is big enough to hold the sky. Her forehead touches the glass, her nose presses against it. The golden fields blur into wide emptiness.

She doesn't know if she is happy. She is not fully happy. She has tasted more than she has tasted yet, but she is not full.

They sit at the table. Jacqui and Rachael dance. He touches her hand with his. And she puts her hand on his thigh. And he kisses her, and it's a hard kiss, a kiss just on the edge of what she wants, and she feels the spinning start, there, as she kisses and thinks why did I do that, and his stubble scratches her, and his hand slides up her thigh.

The train swoops over a bridge, and a gap opens below.

She likes him. She thinks she likes him. He feels like a missed meal, a lack, a hole in her. She remembers his fingers, the flicker of them at the edge of her pants. She imagines him pulling at her more. Taking her somewhere. She remembers the nugget of fear, the click of his teeth on hers as she mishits the kiss. She does it like it seems it has to be done, but it feels almost violent, too, like a blow.

Forests rise on either side, then fall away.

She saw Rachael in the toilet at work later that next day. Rose washed her hands. Rachael stared at herself in the mirror as she fixed her mascara.

'Did you have fun?' Rachael asked. Her face was tight as she concentrated. No smile, no frown.

Rose shrugged.

'Make your fucking mind up,' said Rachael.

The trolley passes. Rose eyes the chocolate.

On Monday, the first day of the penultimate week of the summer term, Dillon has Media last lesson of the day. The sun is bright, the classroom muggy and soporific. On the desk his hands are smooth backed, boyish, until he clenches and the veins stir and pop. He turns his arms, tries to trace the muscle in his wrists and forearms.

His dad's hands are wide and meaty. Same thumbs, though.

'Dillon?'

He looks up. He focuses again on the board. An image of a smiling woman washing up.

'Connotations?' asks Mr Bradman.

'Washing up?' he tries.

The class laughs. Mr Bradman smiles.

'Anything else?'

'Clean?'

Laughs. Mr Bradman smiles less.

'Come on.'

Dillon shrugs. 'I don't know.'

'Femininity?' says Dani.

'What kind? Out of Friedan's three images?'

'Motherhood,' says Dani.

Dillon back to his hands. He traces a vein with a finger. When he prods at it, it gives under his touch.

'OK. Twenty minutes. Write as much as you can.'

Dillon pulls his pad from his bag. He glances over to Rose. She was away all last week. He hasn't spoken to her because they don't speak in school. He wonders how it was.

His eyes flick back to the image on the board. The woman wears gingham. She seems very happy to be washing up.

He starts to write.

At the end of school, he messages Alisha.

where u?

His phone bings.

headache

And then: *heh heh*

He heads down the path. The air is fresh, with the hint of wind growing just on the edge of the warm sun. He can smell mown grass. His T-shirt is loose. Summer touches his skin.

Rose is at the gate. She's standing on one foot, the other hooked around her ankle. He gives her a brief smile.

'What are you up to?' she says as he walks past.

He turns, stops. The sun is behind her. He can't see her face. He takes a step to the left. The light breaks through the curtain of hair to one side of her face. He squints into it.

'Do you want to go for a walk?' she says.

'Sorry?'

'A walk.'

She moves closer, and the sun hits her sharp cheekbones. Her eyes narrow, the hint of a smile. She looks like she knows something he doesn't.

'OK.'

They fall in step together, walking towards the bridge.

'Was London good, then?'

'Yes.'

He waits for the detail. She says nothing. So he asks, 'How?'

She shrugs. 'It was weird.'

'Weird good?'

Another shrug.

The stone buildings of the high street are clear and sharp. Flowers in hanging baskets by the Coachman. They pass the supermarket and the bus stop.

'Are you OK?' he asks.

'Are *you* OK?' she asks. She's almost smiling, like it was a joke, but also not.

'I don't know,' he says.

He doesn't.

They reach the bridge. They drop down the bank at the side and join the path. Dillon checks behind him, under the arch. No one is there.

The river flows fast. The field beside it is lush. The path is dry, and the smells in the air are mostly summer, pollen, the sting of green, the warmth of dusty leaves. A tiny hint of dirt under it all, dog shit, something dead.

The farther they go, the stranger it becomes. Walking without talking. Both know it wasn't normal for her to suggest this. Both know the farther they go, the more they are saying.

The path passes under the first of the trees. They follow. Rose's arms are white gashes in the deep green forest. Her hair bounces as she walks.

The path bends up, away from the river. The sound of the water changes, muffled through layers of leaves. The path bends around the hollow of rocks. Against one rock is a semicircle of stones, filled with dull grey ash and stranded fragments of burnt sticks. The path narrows. Rose walks in front. He can see the effort in her, the way her spine moves, her whole body tilting and bending as her long legs stride. She is close. He can see the way her T-shirt shifts against the tight muscle of her thin back, the dampness at her armpits and in a growing line between her shoulder blades. The smell of the forest is rich and bitter, hot leaves, rising dust at their feet, sweat reeking from the neck of his T-shirt as he bends forward.

It's a challenge, now. A challenge to not say a thing.

The path rises. The trees are spacing out. He can see between them to the edge of the moors. The wind licks in, cool and fresh, and the sun falls brighter between the trees. The bracken is lurid where it catches the light. They come to a wall, and a stile, and they pause, and for the first time in half an hour they look at each other.

Her face is red. Her hair straggles back. Her eyes glitter.

He smiles, a sudden crack of pleasure, and she smiles too, and they know it, they definitely know it, that this is real.

They cross the stile. They walk over the wide moor. The heather is purple, an impossible colour. The wind is hot and raw, the sun harsh on the skin. The path is double tracked now, and as they walk, Rose grabs Dillon's hand.

Her fingers are dry and warm and strong. Their arms stretch between them and their legs raise pollen in dusty clouds from the heather.

'Hang on,' Dillon says.

His words fall strangely. He blinks like he's waking from something.

'Sorry,' he says.

He feels incapable of speech. Like he's been silent for so long he's forgotten. The word 'sorry' sits lumpish between them.

The sun is hot. He lets go of her hand.

'I need a slash.'

He walks away. His feet spring high. He feels light. There's no shelter, so he stops after twenty metres or so. He pisses onto the heather.

He can feel her behind him. He imagines turning round and she's gone. The thought sends a chill down his spine, half terror, half relief.

He squints into the sun.

'Having fun?' she shouts.

Her voice is loud and loose and happy. He shakes the last drops out, grinning.

She stands waiting as he walks back. It seems a long way.

'Which hand did you use?' she says.

'Both,' he says, holding them up in the air, grinning.

She grabs at one, and he lets her.

They walk.

He can feel the swing of her arm pulling at his. He can feel the sweat starting between their palms.

'Did you meet the queen?' he asks, light-headed.

She shakes her head.

'Did you buy me a jacket with gold buttons?' he asks.

She shakes her head.

'Fuck you!' he says, delightedly.

She laughs.

At some point they arrive. It isn't anywhere in particular. They sit. They sit so they touch. Her thigh touches his and he holds her hand with both of his.

He tries not to move. They are just out of the wind, and the air is slow, peaty, warm.

He turns his head towards her, feather-light and full to the brim. He rests his forehead on her cheek. She smells of soap, and underneath it, sweat. His head moves, pushing in. His nose presses under the curve of her jaw. Bees hum over the purple flowers, and he feels the prickle of the heather at his back, under his thighs.

The feel of her skin against his. He could sink into her.

The world holds still.

A sharper buzz startles him. A thought drops.

Should I kiss you?

He knows he should. He knows this is the moment. He turns his head and kisses her, and she kisses him, and she tastes the sweetness of the air inside him, and she opens her mouth wide, and he does too, balancing carefully on the moment so as not to let it spill.

Rose breaks off when he starts crying. She lifts a hand to her lips. She can feel the wetness of his saliva, and a salty trace of his snot.

The only other person she's kissed was in London, and this didn't happen.

Dillon has bowed his head and curled away from her. She puts a hand to his shoulder, but stops before touching it.

'Are you OK?' she asks.

His back heaves. He lets out a snort.

'Are you OK?' she asks again. She wonders what you do. She sits back, wraps her arms round her knees, and watches.

Beyond him a crow rises over the moor, rising on the lift of the quickening breeze.

His breath catches and a sob rips out, and then he stands, and walks two steps and stops. His shoulders are rolled forward, his arms hanging loose but away from the body, like he is soaked in something vile and doesn't want to touch himself.

'Dillon?'

He's facing away from her, but he can't stay still. His body is turning one way and then another, like he's trapped. He's making an odd sound. Eventually it bursts out in a high-pitched yelp of rage, and he kicks at the heather in front of him, and the pollen rises. He makes the noise again, and then he shouts.

'Fuck!'

The sound is sharp and loud and fades across the flat moor.

Ahead of them, behind a rocky outcrop, a bony head pokes up.

Rose shouts in relief. 'Aaron!'

Aaron gets up. Rose sees Dillon frozen with surprise, a desolate look of utter humiliation on his face.

Dillon's cheeks are still tear streaked and his nose snotty. Aaron sits on a sill of rock. Looks at them both without comment.

'Smoke?' he says.

The rock forms a nook, facing the sun, sheltered from the wind. Aaron has made a little nest for himself. His coat spread out. Tobacco and papers scattered on it. He holds a joint in his hand, unlit. His face is sharp and almost old. He's at home, here on the moors.

They pass the joint between them. Dillon's face is drawn and strange. He sucks on the joint, coughs. His cough seems half a giggle, half a sob.

He sits, and then exhales, blowing out through pursed lips. He has passed the joint, but he still inhales carefully, and exhales again. He closes his eyes for a second, and when he opens them he looks at Rose, and then away again.

'Why did the baker have brown hands?' asks Aaron.

Rose is trying to be serious and pay attention to Dillon, but she knows this one and she's laughing already, and the weed catches her, and she's giggling and spluttering as Aaron says, 'You've got to answer.'

She giggles. 'Why?'

'Because he kneaded a poo!'

The giggles rise up inside her in waves, helpless as Dillon looks more and more confused.

'Kneaded,' she says, making the motion with her hands.

Dillon's face creases. The weed catches him now too and he giggles, sniffs, giggles. Aaron howls at how long it took him. Waves and waves of laughter sweep away all the weirdness and replace it with the pure delirium of a summer day.

When they come down, two hours later, picking their way through the forest, across the meadow, back to the bridge, Dillon simply looks tired. Young too, puffy faced and boyish.

They say goodbye at the bridge. If Aaron wasn't there, she might have hugged him. She might have kissed him. Instead she only smiles at him, a lopsided smile that echoes Aaron's. She will hug him next time.

When she's gone, Dillon watches the slick flow of the river. Rocks don't break the surface here, but the turbulence is visible in troughs and eddies as the water piles against the stone of the bridge. The light glitters on the water in nervous flicks and starts.

The clouds move fast today. The wind is rising. It clips the top of the houses, and swirls down side streets. When he was younger, when he was in the main yard with the lower-school kids, on days when the wind rose and whipped round the corners of the old block, a kind of frenzy descended. Everyone felt it. You could see the teachers standing alert, and knots of kids would start to sweep across the yard like leaves. The little ones became hysterical with excitement, and the older students, the year tens and elevens, they sensed the chance for mayhem.

There are things moving in him he can't name. Surges and shifts. They might be emotions, but they feel more physical than that. They sit in his chest and his gut; they shake in his legs. He wants to name them, but the names don't fit. He wants to say he's in love with Rose, but the words flit uneasily on the surface of something fast and rough and elemental. She almost repels him. She feels raw. There's a catch to being with her, a gag somewhere deeper than his throat.

He can feel the sensation of his forehead against the crook of her neck. His tears on her skin. He is exposed.

He remembers the feel of papery yellow skin. A hand in his, smelling of hospitals. Veins, thick and ill.

He turns towards home. He stops as he passes the long block. In the daylight you can see in at the door. He picks his way past the rubbish. Long grasses and nettles rise above it, swaying. The nettles are clustered and seedy, curling at the edges. The door frame lists slightly. Around the base of it grass is growing through the concrete.

He steps inside. The diamond pattern on the wallpaper is faded. At night it looked blue, but in the daylight it is reddish brown.

He backs out. Suddenly he can't be there anymore.

On his own doorstep, he stops again. The gravel path is neat and weeded. The door frame is painted black. At the bottom, though, where the wood meets the concrete, the paint has cracked and the green of moss has begun to take hold.

It has been eight months now.

She's dead, he thinks. *My mum's dead.*

RICHES

Mr Bradman is the first to see it, on the Monday evening. He follows a few media people on Instagram, and the post crops up in all their feeds. People like it. They share it.

By the time he gets to school on Tuesday, other teachers are talking, and the students know too. This is all before she gets in.

The teachers love it, by and large.

'Incredible.'

'Can't believe it.'

'Well done her – how amazing!'

'Have you seen? Isn't it lovely!'

Some are shocked.

'Bloody hell. I thought she was still in year nine.'

The students pretend not to believe it.

'That's not her!'

'Fuck off!'

But like everyone else, they love the story.

When she arrives, the conversations are all about her. She buzzes in at the door to the sixth form café, and talk stills for a second, before someone wolf-whistles, and then someone else shouts, 'Shut up, dickhead!'

And then another person claps, and more do, and people whoop.

Rose shrinks. Her head goes down and she walks hurriedly down the corridor. She leaves at lunch, and isn't seen until Friday.

In the corner of the café, Dillon is sitting alone. He hears the noise, but doesn't look up, doesn't see Rose. Alisha steps over. She pushes him on the shoulder.

'Hey!'

He raises his head. His face is strained.

'You OK?'

He nods. He frowns.

'What was all that about?'

'You're joking me,' she says. 'Are you some kind of social retard?'

His expression doesn't change. Alisha feels a flicker of worry, but she is too excited to pay it any attention. She taps her phone. Dillon leans in.

A beautiful girl on a red carpet. She's turning, and her dress is lifting. The dress is short, glittering, and her legs are long. One sandalled foot rests lightly on the ball, the other rises from the carpet as she turns. Her eyes meet the camera. She's wearing makeup. Not enough that she's unrecognisable, but enough that it takes a moment before Dillon says, 'Rose?'

It's an answer, of sorts, to that old question. Yes, she is beautiful. She looks effortlessly glamorous, but her wide eyes stare back with the same disconcerting blankness that they've always had. Only, under mascara, on that face, in that dress, it's not the same. She has a coolness – strange, mocking and aloof.

She's there. He has to say it to himself. It's hard to believe. *This is her.* He can look. He is allowed to look. He can see the line of the skirt crossing her thigh, the shadow of her collarbone. He can see more than he ever has, and yet she seems to recede before him.

He shivers. He closes his eyes for a second and smells sweat, heather, peat, unwashed hair.

He opens again to look. She looks back.

Did you think it was that easy? she seems to ask. *Did you think that was real?*

Underneath the image it says, simply, *#whosthatgirl*

Underneath that are a string of replies and comments. The names are familiar. The numbers are astonishing.

'Do you see that?' says Alisha, her eyes blazing with excitement. 'She's fucking famous!'

'She's fucking full of it.'

Gracie is having a cigarette at the bottom of the drive.

'She won't fucking talk to anyone.'

There's a knot of them. Alisha is there too, but she isn't friends with these girls. She listens.

'How did she get on the fucking red carpet?'

Ceri Michaels is the central figure. Her hair hangs long and impossibly glossy. She draws immaculately on her fag. Gracie, Jovana and Kelly surround her.

'I think it's fair enough,' says Ceri. 'Good on her.' She smiles brightly. 'Doesn't stop her being weird, though.'

'Do you remember when she came to school in red heels?'

'It's not her that's weird.'

'So that's not weird?'

'It's her freak brother.'

Kelly laughs. 'Oh my god. Did you see him on Saturday night?'

Alisha's trying not to be too interested. These girls are idiots. But she saw Aaron on Saturday, and it was funny. He was staggering around outside the Coachman trying to get in. There was no way they would ever let him in. He kept trying. Eventually he puked on one of the bouncers.

She imagines Rose on the red carpet. She and Oni used to talk about this kind of thing all the time. They used to pose for Instagram, playing games about who could get the most likes, and they used to joke about how one day someone would find them. They would be discovered.

Everyone thought like that, though. Whenever you got likes, or something you said was shared, it felt like it could be the tip of an iceberg. Like there was this parallel world, a shimmering realm of fame and money just round the next corner. It was all rubbish, of course. But every social media star you followed had the same story. They were ordinary until they weren't. And everything became wonderful.

Alisha knows that Rose must think like this too. She knows the fear is real, the shyness real, but she also knows this is something that can only be good, and that for Rose to not give a little back to everyone is just a bit rude.

'She shags her brother, you know.'

Alisha snaps back to the moment. 'That's bullshit.'

They turn. 'How do you know?'

Alisha frowns. 'People don't do that.'

'There's something weird there. She's never had a boyfriend.'

'She's got no friends. How would she have a boyfriend?'

'Look at her. How would she not!'

Alisha grinds her butt into the grass and gets up to head back in. 'Just leave her be.'

That evening the likes have doubled. Alisha keeps refreshing it and seeing the numbers go up. She sees Rose, dark eyed, looking over her shoulder. Sees her dress falling, just so. Sees her legs, elegant and smooth.

The first time Alisha put on makeup was with Oni. They drew big panda eyes on themselves. It was intoxicating. If you pretend to be something, you're halfway there already. Sometimes the whole way.

Alisha refreshes. Sees Rose, Rose's eyes.

She's already different.

A knock on the door. Paula's struggling with the staffing allocation. How to fit the staff you have into the demands of the curriculum you want. Twenty-six lessons per teacher, less for those with additional responsibilities. Then students choose what they want to study, at GCSE and A-level, and you have to readjust. Sometimes people have to go.

'Come in.'

Will Bradman pokes his head round the door. 'Have you got a moment?'

She folds the A3 sheet away. 'How can I help?'

Will hesitates.

'Sit down.'

He does.

'You know Rose? Who went to London with your friend?'

She does. He starts to talk. It takes her a while to unpick

the elements at play. He starts at the end, then cycles back to the beginning. She has to ask him to clarify some basic things.

'Her photo was put on social media?'

'Yes.'

'When?'

'Three days ago.'

'And when did you become aware of this?'

'That's what I mean. Three days ago.' He gives it some thought. 'Monday.'

'And all the students know?'

He nods.

'And her carer?'

'I don't know. I presume so.'

'You didn't tell him?'

Will is startled at that. 'No. Should I have?'

Paula makes a small movement with her mouth that expresses (in her mind) yes, you bloody should have. But it pays sometimes to hold back.

'And now someone has put another photo up?'

He nods.

'Same site?'

'No. This is separate. Another student showed me. It was doing the rounds on a closed network.'

'So, not public?'

'A lot of people have seen it.'

'Can I see?'

He hands over his phone. 'It's not unusual. I mean, I know the kids do this kind of thing. I just . . .'. He looks worried, like he's only now realising he should have been paying attention. 'It's been photoshopped,' he says, nervously.

'Yes. I can see that.'

Rose's elegant, carefully made-up face, glancing over her shoulder, is superimposed upon a splayed body with a fist disappearing into a shaved vagina.

'And who posted this?'

Will made a helpless gesture. 'This is a screenshot of a post, and I can't see the name on it.'

Paula sighs. 'We'll find out.' She opens her laptop. 'Will you send me an email with all the details, and the image. Copy in George.'

Will stands.

'Thanks for letting me know,' says Paula.

She looks absently at his broad, sheepish back as he goes. Then she turns back to the staffing.

'Have you ever seen a dead body?' says Jack.

The wet stones of the bridge arc above Alisha's head. The day has the mulch of weeds and river water in it, stale cigarettes, clothes with smoke, mint chewing gum with smoke.

'Yes,' says Aaron.

Everyone stares at him.

'When?' asks Jack.

Aaron looks like he always does, off kilter and at odds with his own limbs. His trousers are too short and you can see thin ankles above his trainers.

'I saw my gran.'

'In hospital?' asks Alisha.

He shakes his head. 'On the sofa.' The end of the shake has left his head at the wrong angle. 'We had to throw it away.'

He draws on his joint while everyone watches. Alisha waits for Jack to ask another question, but he doesn't. No one does.

Aaron flicks the butt into the river.

'Shall I skin up?' Alisha says.

Jack nods. Her fingers sift through the weed as it sits in the paper, mixing it with tobacco. She likes to see the deftness of it, the skill she has acquired.

'Do you remember when you fell in the river?' Jack says.

She looks up. He's smiling.

'Yes,' she says.

'This river?' says Callum.

Jack laughs. 'It was fucking hilarious.'

'It was your fucking fault,' says Alisha, but she's laughing too. She doesn't say, *You pushed me.* She doesn't say, *I thought I would drown.*

'She properly went in. Absolutely soaking,' Jack says. 'You should have seen her face.'

Alisha licks the line of gum carefully.

He puts his arm round her. 'I am sorry, though.' He squeezes.

She curls the paper round, presses it down, twists the end. She puts it in her mouth, burns the paper tag with a lighter. Draws in.

It was when they went out, last year. They were down at the arch, and they were mucking around, and she said something he didn't like, and he was pretend angry, but also angry, and she was pretend fighting back. But also scared she was going to get hurt. And then he paused, and she paused, and he smiled, and she smiled, and he shoved her in the chest – the heels of his palms at the top of her breasts, so there were bruises the next day. He shoved her, and she fell back, and into the freezing water, and everyone gasped and laughed and shrieked, and they pulled her out.

She lay there, soaking, on the grass, her heart racing, her breaths coming so fast she thought she was going to pass out. Everyone was round her, and they were staring, and you could see it was one of those moments where no one knew what had happened – if it was funny, or bad, or whatever. And she knew – it was in a fraction of a second, but she knew – that she had to laugh. She could barely think, but she knew she had to laugh because if she didn't laugh then he'd just tried to kill her.

So she laughed. They all laughed. He said sorry. He said, *Sorry, but you should have seen your face.* She laughed, and hit him, a mock hit. He kissed her. But she messaged him later and told him to fuck off and die.

Alisha exhales. Jack's arm is still around her.

'Aaron!' Rose's face is silhouetted against the sky as she leans over the bridge, calling.

Aaron starts for the path. Callum reaches out a hand to stop him. His arm is broad. It surprises Alisha sometimes just how *big* boys can be.

'Come down,' Callum calls. Mocking.

Rose hangs, tentatively, waiting. The light behind her makes her neck thin and the head above it sway delicately.

Callum winks broadly at Jack.

'Come down!'

The two of them stand, legs wide, teeth glinting.

Alisha steps towards Aaron, and tells him, 'Just go.'

Aaron stumbles up the path.

Jack's laugh is a sharp bark that echoes like a shot under the bridge.

It seems to Rose that she'd never seen herself before she came to stay at Graeme's. She remembers staring in the bathroom mirror, her face framed by toothbrushes and the towel rack behind her. She would turn her head, and her eyes would stay still while the face shifted around them. She would rub her face in her hands, look close at the blackheads stippling across the bridge of her nose, the red in the corner of her eyeball, the flecks of plaque on her teeth. Her face was a map of textures, of contours, of felt experience. It wasn't beautiful or ugly. Sometimes she pulled her lips back to see her teeth set into the bone of her jaw. She felt her eye socket, felt the bones of cheek and skull. She put a thumb under her chin to feel the gap behind the bone.

Sometimes she makes faces at herself in the mirror still. She looks at herself and tries to see past the gaze of her own eyes. Like she could trick herself and catch herself unawares, see herself like she was seeing a stranger. When she watches other people on the street, in school, their faces are self-contained, closed in on some kind of certainty. Their expressions are true and fluent, even when they conceal or lie. In the mirror, Rose is always haunted by the mocking conviction that she is faking it.

Here is another mirror, though. Graeme has printed it for her. A photo that fits her into the contours of a dress, a turn, two dark eyes thick with mascara and the props of a red carpet and a hashtag. And it looks like a stranger. It is a stranger.

Most days she wears the same jeans. They fit her, falling easily into the same folds, smelling comfortably of herself. They feel like part of her, like a skin, but a skin that protects. There's a tool on Photoshop where you can *feather* – where you can make the edges of an image blur so it doesn't seem so sharply cut out. Her clothes, her habits, they all blur her into the world, letting her fade into the background.

Only now her edges are sharp. The skin of her clothes is one that reveals instead of protects. Her T-shirt contains the ghost of that dress, her jeans the echo of her bare legs. People are looking at her in a way that she can't control. She can feel the eyes on her, probing for things she didn't mean, and can't see. Touching her like cold air on bare skin.

When she thinks of it, a caffeinated thrill runs through her, unsettling and exciting.

Rose comes back to school on Friday. She leans against the low wall by the gate. Normally she would have gone in and sat down, but she doesn't want to go into the café.

Leaning against the wall feels odd, though. She doesn't know how the girl in the photo would lean.

Behind her, on the other side of the fence, the younger kids zip and shriek around the yard. Sixth formers wander up from the road, buzz in at the side gate.

They look at her as they pass.

She keeps her eyes down. Then she thinks they're staring, and she knows she should look up.

'Hi.'

Yannis has stopped.

'How was London?'

His face is lopsided with a serious yet charming expression – wry, but humble.

'Good,' says Rose. He looks weird, she thinks. This is weird, she thinks.

She smiles uneasily, and then stops as he grins at her, a flash of teeth and an appreciative crinkle of the eyes. 'I saw!'

She holds her face steady.

As he goes, she has a sensation of floating, the dip and lift of the stomach as a rollercoaster passes the slow peak of its climb and tips with sudden dizzying glee into the loop.

'Rose!'

She snaps her head round, the swirl in her stomach tipping again.

'You go girl!' says Ceri, enfolding her in a hug.

Her hair is in Rose's face. It smells of coconut. The rollercoaster dips and swoops.

Ceri releases. 'That photo is *amazing*!'

Rose smiles again, tentatively. Rose waits, holding it. Ceri reaches out to give her a brief touch on the arm, another flash of teeth, and then she's gone.

Rose waits, in case she's coming back. She can still smell the coconut on her cheek. She feels unstable, as though she might really be Ceri instead of Rose.

'What a cunt.'

It's Alisha, standing beside her, watching the cheerful bounce of Ceri's trainers as she rounds the corner of the building.

'She fucking hates you,' says Alisha.

Rose blushes.

Alisha laughs. 'You know it.'

Rose wants to joke about something, a quick joke to show she gets it. The words don't come out, though, so she smiles again, her eyes anxious. Alisha stays where she is, though, standing companionably beside her.

'You're really lucky,' says Alisha. 'You know that?'

'Yes.' Like it's only just occurring to her.

'And you deserve it,' says Alisha firmly.

The temperature hits an unusual high. The town is filled with a deadening heat. On the fells, the wind has gone, and in its place is a deep blue sky and fierce sunlight. The heather is dry, and pollen mingles with the zip and flurry of tiny flies.

Rose sits, pressed back into the thin slice of cool shadow against the rock. Aaron sits beside her. Down below, in town, students walk sluggishly into school. She thinks about her picture. She's looked at it so much she can see it clearly in her mind. It looks back at her, confident, mocking.

The heather scratching at her wrist. The gritty stone at her back. The sun, hot against her knees.

Her brother lights a joint. The smoke drifts over her, a denser heat, almost tangible.

A buzzard wheels above them. Her eyes track its dizzying circles. She can see the wings, angling into the updraught of hot air. As she watches, she can feel the looping balance, the swoop of control. Sometimes it seems to be falling, but the sureness of it holds on to nothing and it curls round again into a lower orbit. It goes nowhere. It just rides.

'Do you think Mum saw it?'

She opens her eyes.

Aaron squints. 'She might have.'

Rose says nothing.

'Why not?'

Rose stands. The sudden glare of the sun on her eyes makes her look down. Aaron is huddled against the rock.

'I'm going to school,' she says.

'I'm not,' he says.

Rose walks off across the moor.

She does mean to go. But coming down through the wood she gets a text. It's from Titch. Her name, in pixels on the crappy screen of her crappy phone.

Titch.

The leaves above her glow bright, and the floor of the forest is jewelled with golden spots of sunshine. The light moves sleepily across her skin.

Titch.

Birds rustle in the trees. She hears the sound of acrylic nails tapping across a glass screen. Clack of heels on the rock, whispered breath of the train rushing warm through the branches.

Are you in school?

A slow, puzzled smile drifts across her face, catching with the strange delight of being remembered.

The world swims with sudden unreality. This is a dream, now.

Titch is sitting at a small table by the window in the café by the bridge. Her mouth is a bright red circle round bright white teeth. And she isn't alone. Rose doesn't ask why they're here. This is a dream. In dreams you don't ask.

'You remember Archie, don't you?'

Rose does. Archie sits hunched beside Titch. His dark hair curls slightly. His jaw is square. His eyes are deep and strange and she stares at them until he blinks and looks away. You can stare in dreams. She remembers the taste of his kiss, like coke and aftershave.

'You're seventeen, aren't you, Rose?'

His voice is reedy and southern. She nods.

'You seemed older.'

She says nothing.

'I've been talking to Titch. You saw my post, didn't you?'

She remembers his fingers. His lips.

'I have to say, it wasn't until I checked the photos properly that I realised what I was seeing.'

He leans forward. His hair curls over his forehead with a perfect twist. She remembers why she wanted to touch him. He is beautiful.

In her dream, she almost reaches out.

'You just have that thing.' He turns to Titch. 'That vulnerability. Don't you think?'

Titch nods enthusiastically. Rose drops her hand to her lap again.

'And the way it took off. Did you see the reach of it?' His teeth shine, his eyes shine. 'Everyone was sharing it. People sat up and took notice. The image, but it's also the story – who's that girl? They loved it.'

Titch is practically bouncing with excitement. 'And when they know who you are – where you came from!' She claps her hands.

'I think we can sign you straight away,' says Archie. 'Some pictures, a few posts. We can make something big out of this.'

'Pictures?'

'First a portfolio. Some nice clothes. Post them on Instagram. Then we'll try and book some adverts.'

Rose has known this café for years. Caz used to bring her here. She remembers the day Mrs Jackson took her into the office because she was wearing the wrong shoes, and gave her biscuits. How she asked what Rose had eaten that morning, and what she'd eaten the night before. How Caz came for her, and for Aaron. She remembers the house. Graeme. The space. Sitting in bed, listening to Graeme read stories.

When Caz explained what was happening, Rose didn't react. Looking back, she has no idea what she was thinking. All of those things they had wanted suddenly became real, and all of the things they already had dissolved. She remembers the shower, water running down her face, soap in her hands. The new smell of them. Her and Aaron, they smelt different. They smelt of the new place, and the old one vanished.

'This is big,' says Titch. She reaches for Rose's hand. 'You can have it – everything you want.' She smiles.

Rose thinks of that thatched cottage, the picture in Titch's bathroom. The curl of smoke from its chimney like the lick of Archie's hair.

She nods.

This is a dream.

On the last day of term, they do nothing. Nothing useful. They watch music videos. They talk about things vaguely related to media.

At the end, as they head out, Mr Bradman says, 'Dillon? Have you got a moment?'

He stops.

Mr Bradman waits till the others have left. He sits on the edge of a table. The table creaks.

'Looking forward to the holidays?'

The man's face is kind, his voice gentle.

'Have you got anything planned?'

Dillon says nothing.

'I've been a little worried about you,' says Mr Bradman.

Dillon's flicker of reaction is instinctive.

'Are things getting better, though?'

Dillon nods.

'Good.'

Dillon's face is flat. It's an effort to keep it still.

'If there was something you wanted to talk about . . .' .

Dillon shakes his head. The line of his mouth changes. He's holding his lips tight, but he can't stop the tears coming to his eyes. He looks away, to the corner of the room.

Mr Bradman holds out a hand. Dillon makes no sound, but he can't hold his expression anymore.

'Mate,' says Mr Bradman, drawing him in, one arm across his back, a half-hug, firm, kind.

A gulp, a sound like tearing paper comes from Dillon, and his shoulders heave.

The teacher holds him.

Dillon is shaking his head now, trying to shake away the sobs gripping him.

'Come on, mate.'

At the door, Mrs Jackson pauses as she walks the corridor. She looks in at them, then walks on.

Rose opens a brown, card-backed envelope. She takes the photos out. She spreads them on the table. Aaron reaches for them, but his fingers hover just above the glossy surface. Graeme lifts his cup of tea out of the way.

'Do you like them?'

Rose shrugs, but she's smiling.

Later, she carefully clears a space in the middle of her wall of clippings and tacks the photos up. She looks at them, square and rich and thick amid the tatty paper, then she puts some of the other pictures back, overlapping her own images so they can become a part of the collage.

Her own eyes stare back at her, thick with mascara. She can't look away.

She's on the train again. This is her third time. Trees in thick green banks, houses in sharp, neat rows, the clouds in wide flat-bottomed heaps of cotton-white against the blue.

It seems sunnier than it ever used to be.

She slouches across her seat, her knees wedged against the seat in front. She watches the boy in the seat on the other side of the aisle. He is pretty, delicate featured. Her age. She watches through her hair.

When the train comes into London, she is the first up.

She pulls her bag from the rack. It's a bigger bag than before, but half empty. She intends to fill it. She stands in the aisle, pressed between people, then steps down to the platform.

The boy walks past her. She looks at him, looks down, then up again.

He smiles.

She blushes and walks on.

Rachael takes Rose shopping. This time Rose tries on clothes. First they walk round, and Rachael fingers things, and pulls things out, and spreads the material in her hands, and says things.

Rose doesn't say anything. In her pocket she clasps a wallet that contains a card that will buy what she wants. Her hand is sweaty with holding it.

'Sweet!' says Rachael, in a high-pitched squeal.

'Now that *is* cute,' says Rachael, with certainty.

'OhmygoshIloveit,' says Rachael, in a tone of deep wonder.

Rose watches herself in the mirror, in the changing rooms, and she is changed each time. In a sundress, in denim shorts, in bodycon, she is new. It is dizzying. The clothes feel strange on her, as if they are in some way not permitted. But when she looks, she is not-Rose, and not-Rose is allowed whatever she wants.

She buys things. A halterneck, a skirt, a bomber jacket. She wants to pack them away, but Rachael makes her wear them, there and then, and when she walks out of the last shop she is *new*.

. . .

They meet Archie, in a pub, in the sun, with wide tables, and purple flowers tumbling down aged brick walls, and men in suits with their jackets off and their sharp eyes half closed. He kisses her hand and smiles. When she sits down, her eyes shine, and her cheeks are blotchy with excitement, and her thin knees poke nervously out from the hem of her skirt.

Rose sleeps in the spare room at Titch's. She keeps pyjamas there. Aaron spends his time on the moor, or with Jack.

Rose signs some deals. She signs to an agent, and does some jobs. She isn't suddenly a supermodel, but she does appear in some adverts. On the back cover of a magazine in a short dress springing up in some new trainers. On a sofa with a phone in another advert. She wears sportswear. She uses spot cream. She has an Instagram account.

Aaron cuts her photos out and tacks them up on her wall, next to that first photo, until they cover up the sofas and china shepherdesses.

Sometimes Graeme looks at them. His eyes drift over the pictures. Her limbs, her skin. It doesn't always seem good, this thing that has happened. But when you see her, there, in those places, in those clothes, it does. She looks back out at you, transformed. Beautiful. Like Titch says, it is a fairy tale.

Jack stands back as Callum eases the forklift towards the pallet. The forks slip in, the motor whines, the pallet shifts. The load of timber creaks, moves against itself.

'That's how you do it!'

Callum laughs.

'Slip it in the back before she notices.'

Jack walks round to where the next pallet is waiting. He checks it, notes the numbers on the invoice. Waits.

The drone of the forklift grows louder again. Callum steers a wide arc across the concrete yard. He lets out a whoop. Jack watches him in silence.

Later, they sit, backs to the chain-link fence in the corner behind a delivery.

'Some sharks are six metres long,' says Jack. 'Seen it on the telly.'

Callum leans back, his eyes closed into the sun.

'That's here to where the forklift is.'

Jack pushes his T-shirt sleeves high onto his shoulders. They are satisfyingly brown. He glances over his shoulder.

'All right.'

Aaron walks up on the other side of the fence. He grins into the sun as he comes out from the shaded path. The yard backs onto an area of scrub that leads down to the river. He pulls at his trousers, crouches. Hooks fingers into the fence.

'What a fucking surprise,' says Callum.

Aaron pulls a joint from his pocket, settles down with his back against the fence. Lights it.

'When's your model sister coming home then?' asks Callum.

'I don't know.'

'When she does, tell her she's getting a smashing.'

Aaron sucks at the joint, the hollows in his cheeks deep and shadowed.

'Did you see that picture of her in the magazine?'

Jack nods.

'She never fucking looked like that before.'

'She's OK,' says Jack. 'She's fucking skinny, though.'

'Might break,' says Callum. He grins. 'You didn't ever go there, did you?'

'Come on,' says Jack. 'It's his fucking sister.'

'So what it's his fucking sister! Everyone's someone's sister.'

They lapse into silence.

'Your sister fucking reeks,' says Jack.

'Prick,' says Callum.

'Had to wash my hands in fucking bleach.'

'Fuck off.'

Aaron passes the joint to Callum. He draws.

Jack leans back. Cranes his head towards the boy.

'You ever got any?'

Aaron smiles shyly.

'Come on. Finger or two?'

Aaron makes an odd movement with his head, like he wants to nod, but he can't stop himself shaking it.

Jack winks. 'It'll happen. Just slip one in one day. Some girl, short skirt. Slip it in.' He wiggles a finger, hooked over. 'Keep it bent. Like fishing. Then they can't wriggle off.'

Callum bursts out in a peal of laughter.

Aaron is there at the end of the day too. It's summer, so he has nowhere to be, and no one to be with. Jack and him walk down to the river. They walk to the forest. They take an old coke bottle and smoke buckets in the river water. They lie back in the dank wood, hot with mud dust, throats dry and stung by burnt plastic.

Aaron's eyes drift across the leaves above him. They flick from dark to light to dark. He is waiting. He has been waiting for some time. He waits on the moors, and in the forest, and on the bench outside Tesco. He waits in his lessons, staring at the desk, at the ceiling, at his bony hand. He is waiting for Rose, now, but he was waiting before that. His mind is an eye. His mind is all eye. Drifting attention, and no more. He wants nothing, because what is there to want?

Thirty metres away is the main path. They hear people sometimes, but never see them. A rustle of feet. Once, a dog, a fat-nosed black lab, rooting wetly over the ground, looping towards them, then away, grunting, though the bracken.

Jack feels the earth under his back. He feels his weight. He feels heavy beyond anything. Desire is a weight in his gut and his groin, pressing him down. He wants to drive the forklift.

Aaron rolls upright, hunches forward. His body is too thin. His clothes hang like sails. He packs the foil cup, places it over the bottle. He offers it to Jack. Jack sits up too.

They crouch, knees in the mud. Each in turn pulls the bottle, cut open at the bottom, up so the water draws two litres of dense, acrid smoke. Then they lift and inhale, sharply. Wisps linger. Aaron holds his face tight, screwed in on itself. Jack is impassive, until the smoke eases, dragon-like, out of his nostrils.

They lie back again. The smoke seems to make no difference. In the distance, someone laughs, someone shouts. The sounds deaden and lose themselves in the trees.

'Is she back soon, then?' asks Jack. His mind has been running on Rose. His eyes close sometimes, and she's there, on the beach. In the caravan. Sitting beside him on the narrow fold-out bed.

In her pictures, on Instagram, she moves with confidence. She's a different person. She's not like him anymore. She is part of the world beyond. She looks back at him, over her shoulder. A stranger.

It makes him feel sick, and small. It makes it all real.

'Is she rich, now?'

Aaron shrugs.

It always used to be that everything else was beyond them. The three of them. They were out, on their own, uniquely fucked. Jack is restless. An itch, deep in his bones.

'I passed my GCSEs, you know,' he says.

The sun dapples the ground with bright patches. It looks flat. Jack knows there's more. He closes his eyes. He feels the needle in his arm, the dry calm of the clinic. His head is thick, half dead. He wishes he had a pill. He wishes he was dancing.

'You ever give someone a handjob?' he says.

The words drop unexpectedly. Jack wants them back. They are not him. They are someone older, someone he'd rather forget.

Aaron says nothing. Jack feels the shift in the current of the air though, and he knows he is not Jack anymore. He has come full circle.

'Here,' he says, unzipping himself. 'Give me a handjob.'

The river drifts past. The ground is muddy. The leaves are too still. Aaron moves closer, reaches out. They sit awkwardly, mud covered, stoned, Aaron's bony hand moving slowly.

Everyone tries to work over the summer. Alisha gets a job in Asda. Dillon works at the out of town multiplex cinema.

Every day he smells stale popcorn, nylon carpets and nacho cheese. He hears films muffled behind closed doors.

Sometimes he watches them from a seat at the side or the back.

Grief has uncurled inside him and moves through his body. Sometimes it's in his gut, sometimes his shoulders. Sometimes it wraps tight around his heart and squeezes. When it's at its worst, it grips him at the temples. He can feel the pressure, and the ache behind his eyes. It feels like rage. He's not angry, but his teeth clench, and his fists clench.

One day he walks home, all the way. It takes him three hours. He walks at the side of the dual carriageway as it winds up the valley. He walks on the uneven verge, behind the steel barriers, under the looming trees. Milkshake cartons and scraps of paper have gathered on the edge of the forest, a tidemark of carelessness. Every now and then, he roars. It has to come out, this grief, and all he can bear is to let it out in deep, guttural roars, that rise at the end to a kind of scream, that sting his eyes.

At work, in front of the huge screens, it clouds his vision. It blocks his ears. He won't look at it, but he can't look away either.

At night, his neck aches. It feels like he's held his head still, stopped it from rocking, held tight all day. He drinks water before he sleeps in case the headache is dehydration, then he lies there needing to piss. When he does sleep, he dreams of everyone alive being dead. His dad, Rose, Alisha, Jack, Aaron, Mr Bradman. All dead.

He dreams of Oni. He hasn't thought of her in years. He dreams she is under water. She bubbles like smoke.

He wakes up hungry. It isn't his hunger, but it sits inside him. It swallows his food and leaves him still empty. The thing in him is a hole and a parasite all at once. He feels the texture of it inside him, a roughness, a dirtiness, vast and intimate.

When his dad tries to touch him he pushes him away.

Three weeks in, on his day off, he walks up on the moors. He walks through the forest, up onto the lip of the wide-open heath. He walks across it. He walks far enough that he can no longer see the valley the town sits in, can no longer see anything but a flat, featureless space.

The wideness of it soothes him. There is emptiness here, to match anything he feels.

The summer progresses. The thing inside Dillon loosens its grip a little.

He's sad, now, in a way he wasn't before. He isn't constricted, held, racked by it. It's just there, in the normal way of things, and he can name it.

He speaks to Alisha one night. She knows his mother is dead. But he's never said more than that bald fact. They hold hands. He speaks in phrases that he's heard, that feel like they should be right, but that don't quite fit the particularities of his personal grief.

'I feel like I let her down.'

No, he doesn't. She let him down.

'But maybe I'm angry with her.'

Not that either. This feeling isn't anger.

'No, not that. I just – you regret things. I can't believe she's just – gone.'

He can believe it. That's what is so overwhelming. That fact, that certainty, is exactly what's thrown him.

In the end, the holding hands is enough. The stuttering out of something, even if it's only the faintest outline of what's inside.

If he had the words, he might say that he has as many separate relationships with his mother as he has cells in his body, and they all are grieving in different, often contradictory ways. There are parts of him that despise her weakness. Parts that think she deserved it, that she brought it on herself. That she chose to drink, and that if anything her punishment was not enough.

And then, the parts of him that were formed by her, that exist in the space between them, they cry out. They have no voice. They are a touch, a breath, a daily presence. Language. Love. The tics of accent and perception. They are him, the deepest parts of him, and with her gone, they are bereft.

Sometimes he catches his face at an angle in the mirror, and he sees her. He speaks, and he hears her. He drinks, and he feels her thirst.

She was not a good mother. But she was a mother, and he is still a child, and without her, he does not quite know himself.

Alisha listens, even when he is silent. She loves him. She loves to be needed, too. Close as they have been, he never needed her before, not like Oni did. She cannot say this – to him, or to herself – but there is something wonderful about his grief, the way it sits between them, and they share it.

Paula spends the summer running. She bought some leggings, and yellow trainers, and a sweatband. After six weeks she can feel herself getting stronger. She tries not to run where other people do, although they're hard to avoid. She knows she is not like the young, muscular women she sees running full pelt by the river. She's forty-seven now, and although she is slim, when she sees herself in the mirror she can't help noticing that the line of her legs has a waver to it above the knee. When she runs she feels strong, but she knows her feet hit the ground in a more laboured and tentative way than they might.

She goes high. She finds herself better than she expected at running up hills, and on uneven ground. It seems to make up for her other weaknesses. She runs from the back of her house up quiet streets to where the moors start, and then along a grit road that accesses some farm buildings buried in a fold of the fell. When she gets to the buildings, she runs at an angle down a public footpath, by a fence, the heather whipping her legs on either side. The path leads back round to the road, and she retraces her steps down the streets to her house.

She often goes with the hope that she will work out a problem. She'll set it in her head. But quickly, she finds the effort she is expending crowds thought out of her mind, and she's full of feet striking ground, air in lungs and the cool of wind on her sweaty neck. Eventually she notices what she's really thinking. Instead of a reasoned attempt to figure out how to square the budget, she is speaking to herself in breathless, inane sentences that might have been culled from the interior monologue of a ten-year-old.

Yeah, you're strong.

Come on, you can do it.

In those moments, she finds an image of herself as a fearless, rock-leaping athlete. When her feet strike the ground, she lucid-dreams herself as running for days, never tiring, fleeing and searching at the same time. Obstacles become literal. On bad days, she is fighting as she runs, whirling with a two-handed sword of the kind she used to dream about as a twelve-year-old playing Dungeons & Dragons in the eighties.

Then she stops, and the high lasts for a bit, but she needs to stretch carefully, and she finds the fantasy of strength creaking into stiffness, and she goes in to Andy and a bath.

On the day they return to school, Media is first lesson, and Rose is there. She wears new jeans and a halterneck top. Her shoulders jut out surprisingly, and she looks a bit chilly, but the main thing everyone notices is that her hair is different. It changes her completely. The style is similar, long and straight, but it has somehow been cut in a way that makes it a hairstyle, rather than just hair. And it's clean. It shines.

Dillon didn't expect her. He's seen photos of her online and in a magazine that everyone shared round. There was a story about her – a small one – about the girl who had been found and signed after an Instagram post. When he read it, he felt a pang of loss or of foolishness. It seemed to him like he could have been going out with a model now if he had played his cards right. He didn't, or couldn't, name the deeper current of feeling. It swirled around, a mixture of self-denial, self-disgust and relief.

He'd seen the other photos too. Badly photoshopped. Shaved, slick, lips peeled back, tits hard and high and round, then above, her face. They were lies, but they didn't feel like outright lies. They felt like a fear made flesh, a fear of hard, careless sex and women, better than you, who might laugh at you.

Even when she smiles on a spot cream advert, or laughs at a mobile phone, she seems now like she might laugh at him.

He says hi to her in the Media lesson, then sits far away. He can see her hair. Relief is what he feels, mostly.

They are at the timber yard. It was Jack's idea. He knows the combination for the padlock and how to accidentally knock the CCTV camera on the way out of work so it misses everything. He lights the brazier, pulls off-cut stumps round for seats. Everyone's there. It starts with a few of them, but Callum messages someone, and then more come, and Jack is too drunk to worry by the time he notices there are fifty people there.

'Fuck it,' he says to Callum. 'The buildings are all locked up.'

People from town are there, and people from sixth form. Tinny speaker music fills the circle of warmth. Some people are dancing. Someone has made a bong. People pass a bottle of vodka, a bottle of Jack Daniel's.

Dillon is there with Alisha. She's offered him a pill. He doesn't want it.

Yannis is there. Ceri is with him. She leans into him. He has an arm round her. He fingered her by the chain-link fence before they came in.

Adam is there, who was at school with Callum four years back. He arrives with a scrubby new beard and a pack of beer.

'All right, buddy!' says Callum. 'Long time no see!'

Adam smiles.

'Thought I'd catch up with everyone before I left.'

'Where you off to?'

'Uni.'

Callum laughs. 'Bit fucking old, aren't you?'

'Not so old,' says Adam.

It's dark. It's September, and the night air has a chill to it. The fire leaps high. Dillon and Alisha sit beside it.

'Has it hit yet?' he asks.

Alisha turns and hugs him. He falls backwards. She sprawls over him, tumbles over him so he has something soft in his face and then something hard in his stomach, then she rolls on over onto the ground beyond.

'Calm down, mate,' he says, laughing.

Alisha is flat on her back. She whoops up at the sky.

Across the fire, Dillon sees faces shimmer in the smoke. One of them grins at him. He squints. The half-memory drifts, and then snaps into shape.

'Alisha!' he says.

Alisha's head rises from the ground, tousled.

'What?'

'Look!' he says, pointing.

She drops her head back with an audible thud, but Dillon pushes at her shoulder, urgently. 'Oni's here,' he hisses. He can feel the delay and then the words hit her. Alisha scrambles to her feet.

'Oni!'

A deep call of joy tears up from her throat. She runs round the fire and barrels into her lost friend, arms wide to hug her close. Dillon stands behind. Oni's face is in Alisha's neck. They separate, then they hug again, and this time Dillon meets Oni's eye over Alisha's shoulder, but she's not letting go. He smiles at Oni, but Oni's face is now buried in Alisha's shoulder again.

Dillon doesn't quite know what to do. He feels oddly sad, watching them.

Oni disengages. Now she steps forward and hugs Dillon. Her face is leaner than before, her cheeks less round. Her hair is in a long black weave, no longer frizzy.

She looks earnestly at Dillon, with the hint of a smile remaining.

'How have you been?'

She asks the question like she's an adult.

'Good,' says Dillon. 'I'm good.'

'Oni!' shrieks Alisha and dives in for another hug.

'Sorry,' says Dillon.

Oni smiles. Alisha is embedded in her chest. She strokes her hair.

Alisha throws her head back, gulps down a deep breath and then dives back in.

Oni giggles, and Dillon giggles too, and they feed off each other, until they can't stop and he can see the tears in her eyes.

Alisha stands abruptly and then spins off into a delighted dance.

Oni picks carefully at the teardrops, clears them from her eyelashes.

'She missed you,' Dillon says.

'I missed her.'

Alisha is off, whirling in the darkness. Then she's down, crouching on her haunches, head tipped back. Oni and Dillon sit on two logs by the fire. They are delighted, mostly.

The flames are bright and the smoke drifts heavy and Oni beside him is not the Oni he knew, but Oni *older*.

It feels to Dillon that just being with her he's growing older too. He has a past, now, not just a childhood. All around him the voices and the music and the sound of the fire seem to him the kind of thing he would remember about his youth in years to come. It is a grand, hollow feeling.

And all of a sudden it feels easy to talk.

'Why did you leave?' he says to Oni.

She never told anyone. She just disappeared one day. There was never an explanation as to why she never got in touch, why she left Alisha to wilt without her friendship. Dillon always assumed there was something more to it.

Oni shrugs. 'My mum wanted to move.'

He tries to read her expression.

'Just like that?'

'I suppose so.' Then a warmer, slightly nervous look. 'She hated my boyfriend.'

'Shit!' says Dillon, appreciatively. 'And she moved you away for that?'

Oni nods.

'That is fucking harsh.'

Oni raises an eyebrow. She looks wise, Dillon thinks.

'I didn't even know you had a boyfriend,' says Dillon.

'He was older,' she says.

Older, Dillon thinks. They're all older. The air feels soft and rich and touched with a hint of delicious sadness.

Oni tells them how she's doing an apprenticeship now. Hair and beauty. How she's moved out of her mum's. How she thought she'd come back to see everyone.

Her eyes are fixed on the fire.

'Oniiii!'

Alisha lets the name whine out of her. She's lying on her back now.

The night is dense and strange and Dillon feels like maybe this is it – this is how it works. You talk and you see them, and then . . . something.

Night, and a fire, and music.

'Did we ever go out?' he asks abruptly.

Oni looks at him, in surprise. 'What?'

He's not quite sure what to do with the question now he's asked it.

'I always wondered if you were my girlfriend.'

As he says it, Dillon knows it's a stupid thing to say. Of course she wasn't. He can feel the looseness of his tongue, the beer, the fire. But he also doesn't really care.

'Did you want me to be?' she asks. And Dillon can't quite interpret her smile. Nor does he know the answer. Her black skin shines in the light of the fire. She is pretty. Would she sleep with him? The question drops into his mind, then fades away again. He doesn't know why he thinks it. It just seems necessary.

'You see,' she says. There's a sour twist to her mouth. 'You didn't even want to.'

Dillon feels a gentle astonishment settle on him. He remembers how it was. She kissed him. They kissed. She told him she liked him by kissing him, and he never said anything. He never asked her. And that was that.

He remembers running through the woods with the girls. In his mind, they're always ahead of him. They felt like giants, back then, Oni and Alisha. They knew things he could only dream of.

They still know more than him. They always will, he thinks, but then a memory pricks, needle-sharp, of their young faces, in the schoolyard, in uniform, leaning in as they dare him to come down to the bridge. Their giggles. Their nerves.

It seems so strange to him now that you are young once, and then you get older. Maybe one day he might get used to it. Maybe when you're old, and you've seen the way things are for long enough, it all becomes normal. But right now, at seventeen, in the firelight, the world seems filled with enchantment. With bodies that shift under you month by month, with feelings that strike like lightning and lift you in ways you cannot imagine, or drop you further than you ever feared possible. With looks and glances and half-said words that hit with unexplainable force, and people who act in ways you have no key to.

Rose comes late. People notice her. As she wanders in, they turn and talk to her. She smiles. She's here because they asked her, someone messaged her, said 'you must come'. So she came. She's not certain what she wants out of the evening, but now she's here she walks through the stares tentatively, half enjoying it, half wondering if she should go.

She is wearing new clothes. A dress, strappy. Sandals. A bomber jacket. People say they are nice. Rose likes them. They gave the dress to her after a shoot. She liked the picture from the shoot. It's on her wall at Graeme's.

But when she's there, really there, not still, caught in a photo, she's not the same. She moves more than she used to. Dillon watches her. He sees her hands tugging at the hem of her dress. He sees the duck of her head as she tries to look out from behind her hair. Her eyes look for the other eyes that are watching her. She smiles a lot, and when she does, it's like she's saying sorry.

Once Dillon has seen Rose, the other girls seem different too. Not all of them. Alisha is the same, flat on her back, humming. But Ceri – who is perfect – looks over her shoulder more than you might think. And Xan, tall and Amazonian, pulls at her hair.

And Oni, beside him. He can see the girl in her still, under the weave, behind the makeup. She looks scared.

Jack and Callum watch Rose, too.

'Skinny,' says Jack.

'Still smash it,' says Callum.

'Go on then,' says Jack.

Callum swigs at his beer. 'Can't be fucked.'

Jack watches the circle around the fire. He watches Oni and Alisha. He watches them hug and shriek. He feels his mood darken.

'Who else, then?' says Callum after a moment.

'Who else what?'

'Would you fuck?'

Sometimes Jack despises Callum. He's older. He's bigger. But Jack knows he could fucking destroy him. Something itches in him.

'You're such a faggot.'

Callum grins uneasily. Jack's eyes are hard and unreadable.

'You're fucking full of it. "Smash it." "Fuck it." You're a fucking faggot.'

Callum laughs, but he can't make it as broad as he wants. '*You're* a faggot,' he says.

Jack is on his feet in a second.

'What the fuck you say?'

He towers over Callum. Callum scrabbles to his feet too. He's taller, heavier, but he doesn't want this. They both know he doesn't want this.

'Fuck's sake, man,' says Callum.

Jack pushes him in the chest. Not heavily, but sharply. He knows how to do this. You keep them off balance. You don't let them think. No fear. Because what is there to be afraid of? He's never been afraid, not for as long as he can remember. The worst happened long ago.

'Faggot,' Jack says.

'The fuck is wrong with you?'

Callum holds his hands up, palms towards Jack, signalling calm even as he nervously squares up.

Jack grins sharply.

'You're fucking shitting it!'

Callum hesitates.

Jack throws an arm around his shoulder. 'Jesus, man, I'm only messing.'

Callum laughs. His arm slaps Jack's back too. They settle back down. People around them turn back to their drinks and conversations.

Oni had turned too. She looks a little longer, until Callum catches her eye. She turns back round quickly.

'Haven't seen that one for years,' he says.

'Who?'

'Little black one. Oni.'

Jack leans back, shoulders looser. He is sated.

Callum leans in. He has been scrolling through his phone. 'Hey.'

'What?'

'Check this.'

He holds his phone out. He needs to show this. He should have thought of this before. He's no faggot.

'Look.'

On his phone is a picture. It shows the top of a frizzy head. The perspective is shortened. She's shot from above. You can see the waistband of some jeans, and a sliver of a penis as she holds it.

Jack takes a moment, then he grins. 'She fucking loved that. She used to suck me off under the bridge.'

Callum is momentarily put off, but he scrolls.

'Check this.'

The photo is obscure. Jack frowns. Then his eyebrows lift, delighted. He punches Callum gently on the arm. 'Fucking sweet.'

'She was going out with my buddy. She was up for anything. She stayed at his house for a couple of days, and we got fucked up. We all had a go. He'd just ask her to do anything and she'd do it.'

He leans back, satisfied he's made his point. 'She was *tight*.' he says.

Rose stands. She doesn't want to stand, but she doesn't know where to sit. No one talks to her, because no one knows her. But they watch her.

She wants to go to Alisha. But she can see Dillon beside her, and Oni beside him.

She walks to the corner. She leans against the fence. She sees a figure on the ground. She steps towards it. She knows who it is as she approaches, and the way he is curled there makes her think of another figure, curled in a doorway. She kneels down.

'Aaron?'

He shifts. He's asleep.

She doesn't wake him. But she sits down beside him. She leans over and whispers in his ear.

More people fall asleep, or stagger home. The fire dies down. Rose stays by Aaron. Dillon and Oni take Alisha home.

Jack's mind is slurred. He watches Dillon and Oni holding Alisha, giggling. Their hands interlock under her arms. They touch each other with ease. And Rose. She rests one hand on Aaron.

He feels the dirt inside him. It's in his blood. It's in his touch.

'You OK?'

Rose looks up. A man she doesn't know. Her arms are wrapped tight round her long, bare legs. Aaron is curled up next to her.

The man has a funny scratty beard.

'Is that your boyfriend?' he asks.

'My brother.'

'Do you need a hand getting him home?'

She hesitates. But it's night now, fully night, and Aaron shows no signs of waking.

'OK.'

They shake him. They try to be gentle. He stirs. His head reels up then droops. The man pulls him into a sitting position.

'Aaron?' says Rose.

A groan.

'Come on, buddy.' The man pulls him to his feet, drapes an arm round his own shoulders, holding on to the boy's hand.

'You go the other side,' he says to Rose.

They walk, awkwardly. It's not too bad.

'Bye, Rose,' shouts Jack from across the yard. His voice is hoarse and mocking.

'Ignore him,' says the man.

'It's OK,' says Rose. 'I used to live with him.'

He stops. 'Are you Rose? The Instagram girl?'

'I think so,' she says.

'You *think* so?'

In the dark, she blushes. 'I'm definitely Rose. I think I'm the Instagram girl.'

'You know my ex, then,' the man says. Then, 'Will Bradman? He thinks you're great.'

Rose is about to shake her head, but she pauses.

'Mr Bradman?' she asks.

The man seems reassured by her reaction.

'Do you like him?'

'He's a great teacher,' says Rose, dutifully.

The moon is out, a sliver cut out of the black sky. The three of them shuffle along the road.

'He was my teacher too,' says Adam.

Caz has started to stay round a couple of nights a week. When they wake together the bed smells warm, soft with a night's quiet breathing. Graeme is heavy too, and the mattress shifts and creaks with their combined weight. His curtains are not thick enough, and the light spills onto the cracked ceiling.

Downstairs, she makes tea in her pyjamas. They have pineapples on them. The mugs have brown stains at the bottom. The fridge is old and makes a heavy, rattling hum. Sitting at the kitchen table, they each look down. Her feet are cold, so she lifts them onto his. He says nothing, but looks up briefly.

She doesn't know exactly what she feels. Maybe she has several feelings, all at once, none of them quite compatible with the others. But it's nice to put your feet on someone else's feet.

Caz gets to know Aaron in a different way. She sees him between things. Not there for a careful meeting, soaking up the attention for an hour, or twenty minutes. She sees him bored, aimless. She sees him brushing his teeth.

He walks with skinny, knock-kneed fragility.

She sees Rose too, but rarely. She's always just left, or is on her way somewhere. She has a top cropped high on her skinny midriff, and Caz is touched by the mindless grace of her. She's no older than she was, but she's not in hiding anymore. She has a strappy dress, and dirty trainers. She has a shapeless hoody, and skinny jeans.

She looks like a normal teenager.

It's Rose's eighteenth birthday. Graeme asks if she wants a party. They've never had a party, but he always asks. And she says no, as usual.

Instead they have a meeting. Rose, Graeme and Caz. They have forms to fill in. Eighteen is the start of adulthood, the end of being in care.

She's on her own now.

'You can stay as long as you want,' says Graeme.

Caz has done this before. So has Graeme. You get a feel for the chances. She knows Graeme wouldn't offer this if he didn't trust that it might work out.

'As long as you want,' repeats Graeme.

Caz looks to Rose. Her face is thin, serious. Capable.

'I think that's an excellent idea,' says Caz. She can feel the strange sadness of these moments, for all the hope they represent. It's a victory in a fight that didn't need to have been fought.

One day Rose returns from London, Aaron doesn't go off wandering, and Caz stays round. No one planned it, but they're all there. Graeme orders pizza, and they have it out of the box, sat around the table.

Caz finds herself watching Aaron and Rose eat. She remembers how they were when they first showed up, seven years ago.

For Rose, back then, it was less about consumption than saving up the food. Hoarding. She'd take tiny pieces, stretching the meal out. For every piece that went in her mouth, two or three would go in a pocket, or a cuff, or on her chair to be picked up later. After the first six months, she'd learned. She stopped hoarding things that wouldn't last. No more mouldy corners of bread, or damp chips, or small rancid cubes of chicken. But if she got her hands on chocolate, a bar might last her two weeks, with tiny nibbles taken every night under her bedclothes.

But Aaron eating still holds the faintest shadow of something truly sickening. It's a scar, damage made visible. He eats quickly, not beyond the bounds of what's acceptable, but he does it with every fibre of his soul focused on the plate.

Caz's own food seems less and less appetising.

'Knock knock,' says Graeme.

Rose smiles. 'Who's there?' she says. She has a smear of red on her cheek. Her hair is loose and slightly greasy. She wears her baggy hoody, and in the thick folds of it her frame now seems as childlike as it ever was.

'Europe.'

Aaron belts out a sharp laugh. 'Europe who!' he shouts, his mouth full of pizza.

Graeme frowns theatrically. 'How dare you call me a poo!'

The sudden warmth is palpable. Caz looks at Graeme's stubbled face. His eyes meet hers and he smiles, and she smiles back, a fragile happiness growing inside her.

The studio lights give off a dull heat. Rose stands on a bright white sheet of paper, hanging down from a stand. She feels the heat on her thighs, on her neck. She lets her head droop like she's been told.

'Now up,' says Archie.

She looks up. Her eyes are wide, painted in thick lines. Her lips are red, her cheeks are white. The red is a dark red, the cheeks shadowed underneath, touched with bright sheen along the bone. When they make her face up, she holds absolutely still. They told her to. Even when they speak to her, she doesn't smile, in case the face cracks and falls off.

She goes to change. He stops her, tells her to change where she is. She pulls the dress over her head. She stands in her underwear, ribs moving uneasily with her breath, before trying to pull another on. The makeup artist chides her, holds the collar of the dress clear of her face. Rose stands, stretched high in heels, arms above her head, dress over her face. Then it falls over her. The makeup artist moves in to double check her work. Adjust some hair. She dabs a touch of foundation over the scar at Rose's temple.

Rose goes back to her mark.

'OK. Stand straight on, legs slightly apart. Straight on, like that. Symmetrical. Look at the camera.'

She does.

After the shoot, she walks down the street to the Tube station. She knows the Tube better now. She walks, holding her gaze ahead. Every time she meets someone's eye it feels like they were staring and she's caught them out. The studio makeup is gone, but the makeup artist put some more on, a light touch. She can feel it on her face. She can feel how it makes her look.

She wants this.

Sometimes she has to say it to herself. It's true. She wants this. She's better now than she was. She knows this gives her power.

They call her 'stunning'. She likes that. It sounds like she can freeze men. Lock them. Hold them. And she sees it happening. She sees it in their eyes. It makes her feel strong and weak at the same time.

The street is lined with tall trees, broad and curling towards brown. Men pass her. She can see her knees, and below them her feet. She knows her cheeks are red, and she knows they can't see that. She looks up and sees a leaf falling. Two.

In the woods with Aaron. In the leaves. He liked to play at being in a nest. Anything was turned into a nest. In their house, before they left, they slept in sleeping bags. She curled them round in rings, and then she lay in the middle, with Aaron.

'Watch out!'

She pulls up sharply. The road roars with traffic. A hand is on her arm.

She smiles. He looks at her. She can see how he looks at her.

. . .

There are rules to this new life. Rose is gradually working them out. She's stunning, but she has to follow the rules. Rules about makeup and rules about heels. Rules about following the rules.

This is hard, because no one quite says what the rules are.

They talk so differently here. Not the accent, which is like being on the TV, but the *way* they talk. They say 'of course' a lot. There are a lot of things that everyone except her knows. They know about people, names, places. They know about house prices.

She tries to learn. She finds things out. If someone says a name, she looks it up. They gave her a proper phone, so she can look things up. She looks up 'BAFTAs' and 'Spanx' and 'magnum' and 'caveat'. Sometimes the answer doesn't make sense. She looks up 'Wiltshire' when Titch tells someone about her other house. Then she finds the address in Titch's diary and looks that up. She doesn't know what she expects. She clicks on Street View and she sees it, like in the picture. She leans in close to the screen, and taps the cursor left and right, trying to see around the corner, but it won't go.

In the Street View picture, you can see the roses but not the smoke.

Rose's favourite thing in London is getting off the Tube in Chiswick where the flower stall is. It looks like a film. She walks down the road, and if the sun is shining, the red bricks glow bright, a richer red than bricks back home. She has money now, but still not enough to buy things in the shops she passes. Sandwiches for six pounds. Cakes for five pounds. Coffee.

In each window she sees the ghost of herself, lean and stylish and alien.

There is a shop that sells clothes for babies. Everything is white. The shop assistants are all pretty. The people who shop there are white. The mothers are slim with perfect round bumps under stretched stripy maternity dresses, the dads slouchy-fashionable in brown suede boots and turn-ups.

There is a pub that gleams with dazzling mirrors behind the bar, and acres of space between stripped-wood tables laid out with place settings. Waiters move round in tight black shirts and leather half-aprons. Beers are served in giant wine glasses.

There is an estate agent with rows of pictures. House after house after house, with garages and windows and gardens and sofas, and price tags. She had no idea that people were so rich. She has seen these houses, walked down these streets.

Her face is close enough to the window to look her ghost in the eye.

She tries to imagine Aaron here. What would he say? She wants to show him things. She wants to show him this world, the *real* world.

She walks up the steps to the door of Titch's block. She uses the key Titch gave her. In the kitchen, when Titch is out, Rose cooks. She makes herself a bowl of pasta, adds cheese and salt, and eats it slowly until her stomach is tight.

There are events to go to, with people. She sees Jacqui and Rachael. They hug her. They say, 'Oh my god!' and, 'I love your hair' and, 'Do you want some coke?'

They laugh at nothing. They laugh at her voice, so she doesn't speak. She doesn't know what to say in any case.

She likes to watch, though. Sometimes, she's allowed to slip into the background, and instead of being stared at, she can watch like she used to. Then she sees more. She sees Titch's eyes flick towards her. Titch looks sad, sometimes, and sometimes there's a little bitter fleck in her eye, a glance at Rose's ankles, or her wrists.

She sees Archie, his face soft and eager. The way he waits, smiling, while people talk, already ready to reply before they finish speaking.

Titch calls Archie Prince Charming. He takes Rose out on dates. He wears clothes in ways she didn't think men wore clothes. He kisses her, and sometimes, in the restaurant, he gets her to blow him in the toilets.

When she first kissed him, at the premiere, she touched his thigh in the bar. She reached out because she wanted to. She touches him still, but only when he asks. She doesn't know the rules well enough yet to touch without him asking. The first night there were no rules, or only her rules, but now there are his. She doesn't think he knows this, but it doesn't make it less true.

He holds her hand sometimes, and takes her finger between his finger and thumb. He rolls the flesh, gently, over the bone, like he's measuring something.

He is nice. He's kind. Titch knows he is kind, and she tells Rose as much. He gets Rose clothes and shoes and perfume. When she puts the perfume on she has the feeling that someone else, someone richer and older, is standing behind her. He doesn't ask for anything. He's not like Jack, with wolf teeth and hard, angry eyes. Sometimes touching him is like touching dough. He doesn't feel warm. In the restaurant toilet, she gets cramp.

Titch told him she was in care. His eyes lit up with sympathy. The two of them said she was so brave. Archie said he'd put it on the press release.

Rose asks things sometimes. She knows she gets it wrong, but sometimes she has to ask. One morning she asks Titch if her other house is spare.

'Spare?'

'Empty,' says Rose.

Titch smiles. She smiles when she knows, and she smiles when she doesn't know. 'In a way,' she says. 'I don't get out there as often as I might.'

Rose thinks that's a yes. 'Can I live there?'

Titch laughs. A deep, friendly chuckle. Titch doesn't always laugh like this. She has another laugh for other kinds of conversations. Politer, softer.

Sometimes Rose feels older than them all. But then she reminds herself that she is new here, and she doesn't know the rules yet.

Late at night, Oni calls Alisha. Each of them lies on their bed as they talk. They talk for a long time. Alisha feels Oni's voice in her ear. She hears the softness of it.

'I'm sorry I was so wasted,' says Alisha. 'I wanted to see you.'

'It's OK.'

'You should come again.'

Oni is silent.

'We should go out,' says Alisha.

'I can't,' says Oni.

They talk, long into the deep dark of the night.

In October, Yannis has another party. Dillon arrives on his own. Everyone is outside, at the back. It's cold, but Yannis doesn't want them smoking in the house this time. People drink beers, sit around.

Dillon feels the change since last Christmas. He feels old, and when he looks at the others, they seem older too. He chats, sometimes stands while other people chat. Sometimes stands contemplating his beer. He doesn't like it, but he needs to drink it. He drinks in gulps, the better to feel it in his throat.

He doesn't want to be there. He knows this, but can't say it to himself. He scans for Rose. He looks at his phone to check any messages.

'Dillon!'

Alisha's eyes are big. She gives Dillon a hug. He can feel the tremor in her. She's strung tight on the intensity of some kind of high.

'I fucking love you, Dillon,' whispers Alisha into his ear.

He hugs tight, his arm across her back.

'Come on,' she says, releasing him, then grabbing his hand. They go to where the beers are, then sit against the wall at the back of the garden. She pulls out a joint. They light up.

The smoke thickens in his head. His shoulders relax.

'Fuck, man,' murmurs Alisha. Her head rolls. She snaps it up. 'Dillon, man, I fucking need you.'

She isn't slurring, but her voice is stretched.

'Hey,' says Dillon. 'You OK?'

She shakes her head.

'What's up?'

She carries on shaking, looking down, then pulls her head up, and grins broadly at him. 'I'm good! I'm fucking good!'

He can see something is wrong. He holds her hand, and she grabs his with her other hand, and she fixes him with her eyes, wide and wet and full of emotion, and says again,

'I really do fucking love you.'

The light is fading now. He's wearing a T-shirt, and, while he's not yet cold, the chill of evening raises goosebumps on his arms. The smoke has made him a little sharper, a little flatter. Alisha's hand in his is moving, kneading his. She's a solid presence next to him. It's disconcerting the way she's staring at him.

'Do you want a drink?'

She gulps and nods. 'Get me a beer.'

He stands, but she doesn't let go of his hand.

'Give me a hug,' she says.

He leans down. She holds him tight. Her hair is damp with sweat. She is heavy in his arms. She is strong.

He disengages. He walks out to the bucket of beers. The garden is full of shadows now, and he stumbles on a bottle as he heads back into the house.

He feels a hand on his back.

He turns. Rose smiles. It's a new kind of smile, awkward in a new way. Her teeth are bright, her eyes dark, her hair shiny. She has heels on. They make her loom over him. He can see her breasts at the top of her dress.

'Hey,' she says.

'Hey,' he says.

'How are you?' she says.

She sways gently.

'Look,' she says, holding out her jacket for him to see. 'Gold buttons.'

He smiles. Yes, they are gold. 'Solid?' he says.

'Of course.'

'You got a drink?' he says.

She holds up a bottle. He drinks from his own. She says something he can't hear.

'What?'

She leans in. Her lips are close to his ear.

'I'm drunk,' she says.

He smiles. 'Cheers,' he says, lifting his drink to hers. She clinks, and tilts the bottle back sharply.

She leans in again.

'I could give you a blow job in the toilet.'

He tries to hold his expression still.

'What?'

She's got a half-smile on her face. He has no idea what it means.

'I'm all right,' he says.

Her face doesn't change.

'I'm going to grab another drink,' he says.

He goes farther than the beer bucket, though, up to the end of the garden. He can feel the drink in him, and the night, and the moisture of Rose's words cooling in his ear. He can still see her in the window of the kitchen, talking to Yannis. It's like a screen.

Several people stand around the drinks. Dillon pushes between two figures.

'Excuse me,' he says.

Callum's face clears in recognition. He drops his hand to Dillon's shoulder.

'Hey, buddy!'

Callum's large face hangs open, his eyes slurred. His tongue sits wetly behind his teeth. Jack stands, heavy limbed, beside him.

'Hey,' says Dillon. He feels a flush of adrenaline. Callum's huge, and drunk.

Callum nods towards Rose, still standing at the wide window, laughing now.

'You gonna smash the model then?'

'What?'

'I saw you!' Callum is shaking Dillon's shoulder. 'You're the fucking boy!'

Dillon grins, embarrassed.

'No,' he says, wryly.

'Why not, bud? Everyone wants to smash the model!'

In the window, Yannis is touching her on the arm.

'She's a pricktease,' Dillon says. He's surprised at himself. But he means it.

'Easy, tiger,' says Jack, sharp faced. The mass of him bundles in closer.

Callum crows. 'The boy thinks she's a pricktease!'

Jack's hand is on Dillon now as well. He's buffeted by their bodies. They are laughing, but they are big, and he can feel the sway of drunkenness in them.

'She fucking is,' says Dillon, panicking.

Callum throws his head back and roars with laughter, clapping his hand down hard on Dillon. Dillon staggers.

Jack's face swims out of the dim light, wolfish and sad. For a moment they are inches away from each other. In the kitchen window, Yannis makes his move on Rose. She stands still while he kisses her.

'Fucking pricktease,' says Callum, admiringly.

Dillon knows you can't look inside a person. But you can still see a lot through the chink between one moment and the next. Jack's eyes are hard, and angry, and filled with violence. But they are also, in that fraction of a second, as Yannis kisses Rose, the eyes of someone a lot younger than they seem to be. There is a hurt incomprehension in them, a kind of wounded loneliness.

'You can fuck off, now,' Jack says, sharply.

Dillon smiles nervously, grabs a drink, changes his mind, grabs two. Walks back in the dark to where Alisha sits, his heart pounding.

'Let's go,' he says.

He leads her by the hand back through the garden and the house and out onto the street. The streetlamps have come on, but beyond their yellow light is a deep blue twilit glow.

'It's beautiful,' says Alisha.

It feels like he's walking along the street with a child. Whatever she's taken has pulled her back into herself. She walks with little, flapping steps, like a tired kid on the way home from school.

'You're not like them,' she says.

'Like who?'

'Callum. Jack.'

He feels a momentary stab of annoyance.

'In what way?'

Alisha swings into him, holds him, kisses him hard on the mouth. Her lips press in, and the tears on her cheeks touch his, and the snot. Her mouth opens, and her nose presses into his upper lip, and her breathing comes in starts and sobs, and she is kissing him and he kisses her but her body is hard and muscular and inert in his arms and they stop, standing in the road, faces pressed into each other.

'Sorry,' she whispers, her lips still touching his. 'I do love you, though.'

Jack's dreams are shameful. They wake him, sweating. He lies, in the night, bolstering himself with rage. When his body cannot rest, he rises and does pull-ups. The ache in his muscles tells him he's strong.

At work he lifts too much. His hands are rough. He touches the rough patches with the end of a finger. They feel like horn. They feel like he's growing armour.

He drinks most nights. There's no reason not to. He meets Callum. Callum's a dirty fuck. They go to Mirage, on the pull. He drinks enough that he forgets what's in him, then he takes coke to sharpen himself up again. Girls like him. They like him more than Callum. He dances with them. They dance, their skirts short, their faces drawn on with bright makeup. He leans in, whispers. He touches their slits on the dancefloor. When they're drunk, they let him.

When he fucks, he feels angry. Even when he takes a pill, now, he feels angry.

In his dreams, he sees his father. He sees Rose, laughing, in the bright window.

Pricktease, he thinks. They all are.

When he's working, he feels OK. He lifts, moves, measures, saws. He works hard. Sometimes Aaron meets him at lunch. When he looks at Aaron he sees himself. Sometimes the need to hurt Aaron is overwhelming. Sometimes he does.

When he left school it felt like everything was clearing. But he's back in the woods again. The leaves close over him, thick and green. He needs to find the way out. He needs to ask someone the way, but no one has a map. In his dreams, he screams, and he despises himself for weakness.

He starts running. He goes up to the moor, where the sky is wide. He runs fast. Up the hill, the acid biting in his muscles, his chest aching. He runs until his back is drenched with sweat. He runs up paths, down paths, his legs leaping wider. He makes noises. His mouth hangs open, his brows gathered, in fury or in pain, and the breath drags in and out with grunts and roars. His fists are clenched as he runs.

He stops at the rock, the highest point. The stone stands high, carved by wind. When he stops, his whole body shakes. His breath draws in like sobs. His face is wet with sweat, and tears.

When he meets Callum, or Aaron, he grins, baring his teeth, wide and reckless. He moves. He has to keep moving. When he stops, he sleeps, and when he sleeps, he dreams.

They are the oldest in school now. In class, the compact between student and teacher is different. They pull together. Many students are eighteen now, and they seem like adults. They talk like adults. World-weary, experienced. Unshockable.

In Media Studies, they talk more and more freely.

Rose is often absent, but she is here today. People turn around when she gets in. They smile at her. She doesn't smile back, but her cheeks glow – with pleasure or shame, it's hard to tell. Maybe both.

But Dillon doesn't turn. He still avoids her gaze. She wonders why, out of everyone, he doesn't look.

They are talking about gender. How men and women are constructed in the media. They look at an old copy of *Vogue*. The cover shows an actress, cat eyed, turbaned, full of eastern promise.

'She plays a dancer in the film,' says Mr Bradman. 'A Turkish dancer. What do you think that signifies?'

'Exotic,' says Dillon.

'Sexualised.'

'Objectified.'

Mr Bradman talks. He talks about 1965, about Betty Friedan again, about the roles women played.

'Look at this one.' He shows an image from inside. 'He's doing something, off to one side, fiddling with something.' He points. 'Active.' He points to the girl. 'She's passive.'

They look at an advert. A mother and child, advertising Pears soap. The mother's head inclines down, looking at the child. The child looks at us, secure, happy.

'What does this say?'

At the front of the school, on the grassy bank, Dillon sits with Alisha. Alisha is eating a cheeseburger. Dillon is eating a Big Mac.

'You know that's not healthier,' says Dillon.

'It's smaller.'

'You're just going to be hungry afterwards. You'll eat something else.'

'Twat.'

Alisha pops the last soggy scrap of bun in her mouth and crumples up the greasy paper. She looks for a bin, even though she knows there isn't one, then puts the paper on the grass behind her.

As she turns she sees Rose walking down the path. She turns back to Dillon.

'Princess cocksucker's coming,' she whispers.

'Fuck off,' says Dillon, punching Alisha lightly on the arm.

Alisha cackles. 'Why so sensitive?'

'Just fuck off.'

'Hi.'

They look up. Rose has stopped beside them. Alisha smiles. 'Hi.'

Rose is wearing her old jeans, sandals, and a top slashed at the arms and the back that hangs loose over her lean chest. She looks like she's been assembled out of two different people.

'See you later,' Alisha says, and winks at Dillon. He still has half a burger left.

Dillon and Rose stare after Alisha as she walks back up the path, for slightly longer than they need to. Then they turn back to each other. She doesn't look like a model, Dillon thinks. She looks like Rose.

Dillon takes the biggest bite he can manage.

'How's your film?'

'What film?' he says, disconcerted.

'The film you were making. About the seasons.'

Dillon flushes with shame. He can feel the dark and the quiet of the broken house. He wishes she would shut up. He wishes he could tell her to shut up.

'Have you stopped?' she says.

'Sort of,' he says, keeping his voice neutral and his face low. He takes another huge bite, then crams the rest of the burger in. He scrunches the paper up.

'I met a director,' she says.

His cheeks are bulging. His mouth is dry. He can't swallow.

'In London,' Rose goes on. 'I made an advert. I met the director. He gave me his number.'

Dillon is looking at her in astonishment, his mouth full of Big Mac.

'You can finish your burger, you know.'

Dillon blushes. Looks down, chews. He can see her sandalled feet. They are large and knuckled with ridges of bone. Her big toe is massive. He can feel her eyes on him like an itch.

He swallows.

'You could come down with me if you wanted.'

The smile has fallen from her face. He notices that her cheeks are blotchy, an uneven pattern of red.

'We could go to London,' she says. It's so unguarded, and so needy. It can't be real. Dillon feels a pull in his chest. It's painful looking at her. He wishes she would shut up. He wishes he could tell her to shut up.

He laughs. 'You're all right,' he says.

He hates his voice. He wishes she knew the rules. He doesn't know them either, but he knows this is not in them.

He stands up. She doesn't move. She's close to him. He feels her overpowering loneliness. It's frightening.

'You going back in?' he says.

They walk up the path. He wants to say yes, but she is too

raw. You couldn't know what else she might say or do. She might say she loved him. She might kiss him. He doesn't want that. Not again.

Titch is having lunch with Archie. She's using him for shoots regularly now.

'Is she OK?' Titch asks.

'Rose? In what way?'

The low noise of quiet talk fills the restaurant.

'I don't know.'

Archie is amused. He leans back as their food arrives. 'You'll have to be more specific.' He moves his knife and fork slightly as the waiter places the plate down. 'Thank you.'

'Thank you,' says Titch. They examine their plates.

'This looks lovely.'

Titch tastes a mouthful of her salad. 'Mm,' she says.

She finds it hard to pin down the nature of her concern. She remembers the way Rose held her hand on the Tube that first day. She can still feel the touch of her fingers. She remembers the electric shock of it. She'd drawn back, but then she'd spent all day with the imprint of those fingers, like a burn in the palm of her hand.

'She seems a bit detached.'

Archie frowns. He swallows, then takes a sip of wine. 'She's a model. That's what they're supposed to do.'

Titch reaches for the pepper. 'I don't mean when she's working. I mean when you talk to her.'

What Titch is trying to say is that she feels cut off. Rose was her thing. She'd never done anything like that before, and the first time she did, it changed someone's life. It still feels good, but Titch can't help thinking that somehow it ought to feel better.

Archie says, 'She's sweet. She's a bit overwhelmed at times, that's all.'

Titch thinks through this. Yes. Could be.

'And you two?' she says, her eyes lifting to Archie's face. His features are regular and well cared for. His dark hair waves just right. He's boyish, but the dark stubble gives him a more manly edge.

He smiles. 'All good.'

Titch chases a lone cherry tomato with her fork. When she was eighteen, she had a boyfriend who was thirty-two. She met him when she was an intern at her first magazine. He was a writer. She sees the same thing now. Young, fresh faces, and the more experienced men make a beeline for them. Her mum was horrified. But Titch knew what she was doing. She knew it was a dalliance. She also knew the better she integrated with the social world of the magazine, the more doors would open for her.

It wasn't quite as calculated as that. Nothing ever was, for her. But there are many layers of response. The social world is a nuanced place, and you move through it using deep-buried knowledge. As Titch got older, more and more she was able to name that knowledge, see its workings. At the time, there was just the same amount of social skill at play, but it was instinctive, instilled carefully from an early age. It seemed the most natural thing in the world to flatter, to make people laugh, to highlight their strengths so that they felt good in your company.

Titch chairs many meetings. She knows that ideas take hold in subtle ways. A good manager is a gardener of people. You allow a shoot to grow in a warm greenhouse, then transplant it to the outside world. You feed. You support. Sometimes you force, or you prune. What you never have is an equal marketplace of ideas. There is always a preconception, a personal animosity, a sense of vulnerability or unease that blocks one path and opens another.

After the initial excitement, the thing that has surprised her about Rose is how little friction there has been so far. For someone so unfamiliar with the world she finds herself in, she rarely puts a foot wrong. She seems to move with a blank ease, accepting how things are, and allowing people to read into her what they will. She is lovely. Sweet, as Archie says. Her naïvety is almost overplayed, were it not so convincing.

'So she's happy?'

'Of course she's bloody happy!'

'Yes,' Titch says. 'Of course. She's overcome so many things.'

Archie nods seriously. He takes a sip of wine.

'You can't imagine,' he says.

Titch raises an eyebrow. She wonders what Rose tells Archie, whether she actually says the things that must have happened to her. She's always wanted to ask Paula for the details, but she knows it would be crass.

'Apparently her mother once shut her head in a door,' says Archie.

Titch raises a hand to her face in shock. The noise of the restaurant sharpens in her ears.

'Oh my god,' she says.

'Just awful,' Archie says, vaguely. 'Makes it all the more amazing what's happened.'

Shut in the door, thinks Titch. She feels sick. Her hand is back at her mouth again to catch a stifled half-giggle.

'Oh my god,' she says, 'I'm so sorry.'

'It's pretty extreme,' Archie says, with a smile.

'I'm not laughing,' says Titch. Another hiccupped giggle. She feels a glow of shame. But also shock and pride and disquiet at her own excitement. 'Oh my god, I feel terrible,' she says.

Archie's smooth face droops with sincerity. 'Come on,' he says. 'It's fucking awful.' He squeezes her hand. 'But let's remember this story has a happy end.'

Titch smiles back at him, even though she feels suddenly tearful. 'Yes,' she says. 'Yes, I suppose so.'

Yes, it was a good thing. 'Yes,' she says.

Beyond Archie's shoulder, a woman and the man she's had her dinner with leave their table. Charming smiles as they dance out from behind their chairs. Titch watches the delicate manoeuvre unfold, the hand held out to the lower arm, the lean into a gentle peck on the cheek.

'Yes,' she says, one more time, her voice fading.

She remembers again the touch of Rose's fingers. The breach of it. All the ways we interact, the rules and expectations, all predicated on the fact that other people are just like us. Rose had torn a little hole in that. She wasn't like Titch had been. Not ever.

There was a kind of violence to that touch, delicate as it was. It let in shadows.

'She had to hold my hand the first time we went on the Tube,' says Titch. She doesn't quite mean to say it.

'She is so sweet,' Archie says.

'Oh yes,' says Titch, grateful for the word. 'Such a sweet girl.'

Graeme walks around the forecourt with Rose. The cars gleam in the sun. They are not good cars. They are little bangers for new drivers.

Rose can't drive yet, but she wants to.

They test drive a Peugeot 107. It's twelve years old, and red. Rose sits in the passenger seat. They circle a few blocks, changing stations on the radio. Outside, the town is bright. Even the grey estates look sharp and clean.

Back at the dealer's, they stand by the car. The sun is warm on Graeme's neck.

'Why don't you wait?' he says.

Her shoulders are bare. She's wearing a halterneck. Her skin is pale and freckled.

'Titch says I should enjoy the money.'

'Yes, but why do you need to drive?'

'I'm going to live in the country,' she says.

Graeme feels a pull of sadness. She is an adult, almost, but the way she says 'the country' is the same as how she said it when she first came, trailing the strange myths of her disordered childhood.

'You know you can stay with me as long as you want,' says Graeme.

She can. He wants her to. But it suddenly seems entirely inadequate that a home is something he can just offer on a whim, half meant.

'We're going to do it soon,' she says.

'We?' He frowns. 'You know Aaron has to stay until he's sixteen.'

She seems surprised. 'Why?'

'He's in care,' Graeme says. 'I have to look after him.' He's flustered. He's not saying things in the right way.

'It's my job,' he says. He sees her thin neck bowed. He wants to touch her, hug her, but he can't bring himself to do it.

They buy the car.

She gets lessons, but Graeme takes her out for practice too. He's impressed. She frowns as she drives, a tight, intense frown of concentration. He's never seen her focus on anything so much before. She puts cushions in the back seat. Sometimes she and Aaron sit in it with the doors shut.

They sit there for hours.

Caz sees the frown on Graeme's face settle. He talks less. At dinner, he is distracted.

At night, in bed, Caz asks what's wrong.

'She looks like her mother,' he says.

In the dark, Graeme's mind circles back. He's remembered these things before, vaguely, as something long finished, but now they are vivid again, bright and young as Rose. She is like her mother. She wasn't, but now she is. In the photos and the adverts she is, and now he can't stop seeing it.

He met Ash when he was twenty. She was sixteen. She was friends with Alice, whose brother Frank sold weed.

They met at the park. They used to hang about at the bridge, leaning over the edge to flick fag butts into the river. When they were younger they'd lurked under the arches, but now they were twenty they smoked with a swagger, and shouted a little too loudly to each other, and didn't care who saw it.

Frank would meet them, shake hands ostentatiously and palm a nugget of dry resin. Then they'd walk on down to the shops and get a tenner out of the cash machine for him. Then they'd offer to roll one with him.

That day they walked on from the cash machine to the playpark. There was a sheltered bench there, and no kids went since the swings had been torched.

Ash was with Alice and her friends. They looked young, like they were still children, but not Ash. She was tall, and she had hoops in her ears, and her hair was piled high. Graeme watched her idly as they sat and waited for Darren to skin up. She saw what they were doing and came over. Graeme thought she was going to speak to him, but before she opened her mouth Frank said,

'Fuck off, Ash.'

'Why?' she said.

Frank made a move, a sudden move as if to make her flinch, but she stood there impassively. The first truly beautiful person Graeme had ever seen. A Russian princess in a rusty playground.

In the dark, Graeme feels a sudden revulsion for himself. He's fat, and old, and Caz beside him is just as fat.

The mattress heaves as Caz turns. He closes his eyes and wills himself to sleep.

Out in the car, Rose drives up the narrow road onto the moors.

'Careful,' says Graeme.

She keeps her eyes on the road. Where the incline rises sharply, she snatches at the gears, stalls, and slams on the brakes as she starts to drift back.

'OK, OK,' says Graeme.

Her eyes are wide. There is sweat on the side of her nose.
'Hill start,' he says. 'You can do it.'
One hand on the brake, she eases off. The engine roars too loud, cuts.
'OK, fine,' he says. 'You're OK. Handbrake on.'
She pulls it up sharply.
'Neutral. Now relax.'
She sits back.
'OK?' he asks.
She nods.
'Shall we swap?'
She nods.
They cross at the bonnet. She's wearing her halterneck. Her shoulders are like her mother's.
'OK,' he says.

That night, Graeme heads down to the Coachman. He hasn't been there in years. It's exactly the same. The red and brown patterned velvet seats, the round bevelled tables, the Sky Sports on in the corner, and the deep, steady odour of stale beer and pre-smoking ban fags still leaching out of decades-old polyester fabric.
He can see Frank's back as he hunches forward at the bar. He's bald now, still broad-shouldered. He's not fat, but the skin gathers in rolls at the nape of his neck.
Graeme turns and leaves.

He is in her room. She's out, but he comes in sometimes to look at the photos on her wall. Lying back, jumping. Her arms, long, bare. Her legs, long, bare.

He's seen the other photos, of course. The school told him. They were crude and fake, but they spoke to something he felt was true. It seems to Graeme that when Rose started the modelling, she changed. She became – in those images, real and fake – available.

Or, at least, half available. The two parts of her overlap. The edges blur. Sometimes, talking to her is like having double vision. She's in the same old jeans, but her hair and makeup are perfect, and as she talks, you can see she knows they are perfect. You can see the awareness hanging behind heavy mascara, sitting alongside her normal awkwardness and a strange kind of fear. She knows, and she takes pleasure in knowing, but she is also still a child.

When Rose first came, she was dirty, and she had a sour, nasty smell Graeme associated with old people. She was easier, then. He was better, then.

Graeme watches her as she moves around the house. She's self-conscious in her new clothes, but when she doesn't know you're there, it's like he's watching a movie star. Sometimes he stands quietly in the hall, and if she has her bedroom door open he sees her moving forwards and backwards across the gap. Moving her hair as it sits on her shoulders. Lifting her T-shirt over her head.

There are fewer in today. Dillon. No Alisha. Rose, with bags under her eyes. Six more.

'Queer theory,' says Mr Bradman. 'Judith Butler.'

They take notes as though they really care. He talks about the change in culture since 1965. He talks about progress. He talks about criminal codes, ages of consent. Gay marriage.

'I knew no one at school who was out,' he says. 'But now the school environment is so much more accepting.' He smiles. 'Isn't it?'

'There's lots of people out in this school,' says Dillon to general approval.

'Poppy and Farrah,' he adds. 'They've been together for years.'

People nod sagely. Rose's eyes are big, her mouth a tight line of concentration as she stares at Dillon. He doesn't seem to notice.

'There are a couple of students who identify as transgender, as well, aren't there?' prompts Mr Bradman.

Dani, whose mother is Nikki from the office, says, 'With a boy's name?'

'They would identify as boys, not just by name.'

Dani raises an eyebrow.

'Come on,' says Dillon with a world-weary air. Everyone laughs.

'What?' says Dani. She's a little annoyed, a little flirty. 'What do you mean, "Come on"?'

Rose watches intently. Dillon smiles knowingly.

'I think we're all a bit beyond that.'

'I think he's right,' says Mr Bradman. 'A lot has changed. And it all means that ideas that Butler talks about, such as camp, are not the only way to be gay anymore. You can have gay rappers, gay rugby players. There is less and less of an identifiable "type" of queerness.'

'Like you,' says Rose.

The class is totally still. A second passes, then another.

'Yes,' says Mr Bradman.

He speaks like he's answering any other question, and his face is rigidly normal. A few of them surreptitiously glance at each other. Dillon looks at Rose. She flushes.

'Moving on,' says Mr Bradman. 'Let's see what Butler actually says.'

After the lesson, they all try to take it in their stride. After all, it's no big deal. The only surprise is that he didn't *seem* very gay.

'My brother's gay,' says Georgia. 'He came out when he was twelve.'

Dani is a bit more vocal. She loves gossip. Her and her mother between them know everything that goes on in the school, and she seems affronted that this is news to her. She questions Rose. Dillon listens.

'How did you know?!'

Rose has those red spots of embarrassment or pleasure on her cheeks. She can't stop her eyes flicking towards Dillon.

'I met his ex at a party.'

'A London party? With models?'

'No. At the timber yard.'

'At the timber yard?' says Dillon, now giving Rose his full attention.

'What was he doing there?' says Dani.

'He was in Callum Watson's year.' Rose wants to say more, to keep Dillon focused on her. 'He used to be in Mr Bradman's class in school.'

Dani's eyes widen.

It takes two days for the rumours to settle on someone who reports them to Paula.

'He had a sexual relationship with a pupil?'

George gives a grim look.

'Jesus,' she says. Things are crumbling around her. She can see, in her mind's eye, Will and Dillon, in his classroom, embracing.

'Jesus,' she says.

Next lesson Mr Bradman isn't in. They have a cover teacher for Media Studies. The class sit in a feverish silence. Rose isn't in either.

At break, the cover teacher says Dillon needs to go and see the head. There's a bench outside her office for students to wait nervously on. He waits nervously on it.

'Dillon?'

She's opened the door. Smiling at him. That's worse.

'Come in.'

In the room is someone he's never met.

'This is Mrs Halliday.'

She has blonde highlights and a sharp, lined face. Her expressions are small, bright, mobile, warm. She has a laptop open in front of her.

'Hi Dillon.'

Mrs Jackson is doing her best to look cheerful, but she has a deep crease of worry across her forehead.

'Dillon, we need to ask you a few things. It's important you be honest.'

She presses one finger to her cheek.

'Can I ask you about Mr Bradman?'

Dillon keeps his mouth closed.

'He teaches you Media Studies, doesn't he?'

Dillon nods very slowly.

'How long has he been teaching you?'

Dillon tries to think of a way of not replying, but he has no defence against their two professional smiles.

'He's a really good teacher.'

Mrs Halliday says, 'Of course.' And, 'How long has he been teaching you?'

They are speaking in careful, nonthreatening tones. He wants to tell them to fuck off. He wants to tell them he can see through them. He doesn't know what they want, but he knows they want something.

'Since year nine,' he says. 'I had him for English, and then for Media.'

Mrs Halliday is typing on her laptop.

'And you say he's a good teacher?'

Dillon nods.

'So he helps you?'

Dillon nods.

'And you enjoy his lessons?'

Dillon nods. Mrs Halliday types.

'Do you ever see him outside of school?'

'What do you mean?'

Mrs Halliday gives a short, quick smile. 'Do you see him outside of school? Do you ever bump into him, or meet up?'

Dillon shakes his head no.

'Sure?' asks Mrs Halliday, head to one side.

'I've maybe seen him at the shops?' Dillon offers.

'At the shops?' says Mrs Halliday carefully.

Dillon nods. 'I saw him at Asda once, I think.'

'And so you've never met with him?'

Dillon shakes his head.
'And has he ever touched you?'
Dillon stares.
'Has he ever touched you, Dillon?'
Dillon looks to Mrs Jackson. Her face is riven by concern.
'No,' he says.
'Dillon,' says Mrs Jackson. 'Has he ever given you a hug?'
The floor seems to lurch under him.
'Yes,' he says. He feels sick. 'He put his arm round my shoulders.' His voice is draining away. He has to pull it back. 'I was upset.' He wants to scream but worries he might faint. 'Is there something wrong?' he says.
Mrs Jackson leans forward.
'Dillon, this is a complicated situation. The main thing you need to do is answer our questions honestly.'
'I am,' says Dillon. His throat is tight.
'Dillon,' says Mrs Halliday, 'has Mr Bradman ever made you uncomfortable by the way he touches you?'
The knot of tears gathers at the back of Dillon's throat. He doesn't know how to hold himself. He can see what these two women believe.
'It's not what you think,' he says. He knows what they're hearing is different from what he's saying. He tries again.
'My mum died.' The words are raw. 'I was upset.'
Mrs Halliday has a different expression now, sad and warm. 'What you need to understand, Dillon, is that sometimes these situations aren't so clear cut when you're in them. But there are standards of behaviour for teachers that they need to uphold.' She frowns gently. 'Mr Bradman is in loco parentis. That means he's in the position of a parent, or a guardian.'

Dillon clenches his jaw. He knows what he wants to say, but the words he needs have vanished. He wants to say that Mr Bradman was exactly that – he gave him the time and the comfort his dad should have given. He wants to ask why it is Mr Bradman they are bothered about. He wants to ask if it's all because of what Rose said.

'Can I go now?' he says.

Mrs Jackson's eyes are not unkind.

'I'm sorry about this, Dillon,' she says.

'Can I go?'

She nods.

Two in the morning. Graeme can't sleep.

He remembers being young. Not just remembers, but allows himself to feel it again. A kind of hopped-up, nervy excitement as you headed out. The sense of possibility, of danger without really understanding that danger could be real. The faces of the others – Ash, Frank, Alice, Paula Mason from two doors down. The taste of cigarettes, of weed, of cheap vodka. And laughter.

They laughed so much. Someone splutters over a drink. Someone mispronounces a word. A tampon drops out of a bag. Stupid stuff. But at the time, half pissed, stoned, they creased up. They collapsed in hysterics. It was brilliant.

Graeme can feel it in his bones, surging back through the years. It was his first world, his best world. Nothing else was real. These people were everything, and to miss one night, or to be pushed away from the magic circle, was intolerable.

There was plenty in between. The damp waiting. The conversations that don't spark. The bit where you hang around with the one in the group that you're a bit scared of. The tap out of powder on a hand and the pounding thrill of fear in your chest. It was real, and scary, and looking back, for some of them it was the start of something going very wrong.

But then, on those few nights, those special nights, you do more than laugh. You cry out at the moon and shriek your love for the others. You kiss and hug, and feel the dirt and the rawness of it.

Ash was the queen of it all. When she smiled it was adulthood beckoning. She was experienced. Everyone said so. She was tough. She was old, even though she was only sixteen.

Graeme screws his eyes shut, panic rising inside him.

Driving. Rose shifts smoothly.

'Well done,' Graeme says. He watches the road, alert for dangers Rose might have missed.

'Left,' he says. 'Good.'

They're circling the roundabouts at the edge of the industrial estate. The roads are barely used and empty. The sky is grey.

'Right.'

The car turns. She's wearing the halterneck. Her arms are like her mother's.

'Right.'

In the photos, she jumps, lies, pouts.

'Left.'

The car turns.

'Pull in.'

The car stops.

Rose turns to him. He keeps his eyes on the smooth road ahead, the rough verge. He knows he's going to say something, but he doesn't quite know what.

'You know,' he starts.

But he gets no further.

Really, it's Ash he wants to speak to. He wants to say sorry. He wants to say that he knows now that she was not who he thought she was.

He lowers his head forward into his hands.

'What?'

He doesn't look up at first.

'Should I go home?'

He sits up. Shakes his head.

'What's the matter?'

He looks at her.

'You need to watch out,' he says, clumsily.

'Did I hit something?' she asks.

He shakes his head.

'People will . . .' he tails off. He shrugs helplessly, gestures at her clothes. She's looking back at him, and he feels a sudden chill.

'I don't mean . . .' he starts, but stops again.

Her face is blank, but he catches something knowing in her eye.

'Have you slept with him?' he asks.

'Archie?' she says.

He hadn't meant to ask that. But he nods.

'Yes.'

He swallows.

'You slept with him?'

'Yes.'

'Fuck's sake,' he breathes. He feels an unreasoning anger swell. He strikes the dashboard in front of him with one pudgy hand and it shakes the little car. He's surprised at himself, and he looks up at Rose with a half-smile at his own ridiculousness, but she is rigid with fear.

His face falls.

'Rose,' he says.

She starts the car.

'I'm sorry, Rose.'

She drives on.

Dillon goes to her house after school. He walks fast. He can't put a name to what he's feeling, but it tears around inside him in a fierce rolling boil. His eyes ache, his temples ache. There's a hook of guilt lodged in his gut. Even on an ordinary day, he often feels like he's high up, on a ledge or a tightrope. Now it's like he's falling.

The late October sun is low and still warm. The stone of the high street glows pleasantly. The pavement is hard under his feet.

As he walks, he brings an order to things, and a name.

He is angry. He is angry with Rose.

It's such a relief.

Rose's house. He's been here a few times now and never gone in. He doesn't even know if she's there. He doesn't know what he wants to say, or how.

The house is stone, terraced. The garden at the front is tidy, with bushes in tubs and a gravel chip path.

He knocks at the door. A man answers. He is older, grey-haired. Not old, but older. He wears jeans, a hoody. Trainers. He has a double chin. Watchful eyes.

'Looking for Rose,' says the man. The flesh of his cheeks creases into folds. He winks. It seems to be an effort. 'Ah,' he says. He holds out a hand. 'Graeme,' he says. 'Come on in.'

But Dillon doesn't want to go in. He doesn't know why.

'Will you tell her I'm here?'

Graeme raises his eyebrows. 'OK.' He turns, then turns back. 'Name?'

'Dillon.'

He goes back in, leaving the door open behind him.

Dillon hears footsteps. He can see into the hall. It's carpeted, with carpet that is strange, like other people's carpets always are. The patch by the door where people's feet fall is worn and dirty. The house smells of bacon and air freshener. He can see the living room through the window. There's a telly. There's a large picture of a cow.

Rose steps into the doorway, one hand on the open door. She's in her old jeans, a T-shirt. Her hair is unbrushed. Dillon swallows. She looks like she used to.

'Do you know what you did?' he says, and his voice has a clipped fury to it he's never heard in himself.

Her expression doesn't change. It itches inside him. It makes his skin crawl, like looking at something naked, or skinned. He's never known anyone who looked at him like she does. No defences in place. Yet she makes him feel like the weak one. He's disgusted by himself.

'Do you know what you did?' he repeats, pushing himself further into anger.

A small, confused dip of the eyebrows.

'You've got him sacked.'

Not a flicker.

With a sense of release, he looks at her and finds that no, she wasn't what he thought. He thinks of how easily she changed. How she probably sucked Yannis's cock. His anger is more natural to him now. He reaches for the angriest thing he can say.

'You lying cunt,' he says.

He feels ridiculous. And all she does is take a step closer to him. She smiles at him, a stupid look on her face like she doesn't even know he hates her.

'Fuck off,' he says. She's still moving in. He pushes her with the heel of his hand at her shoulder. 'Fucking pricktease.'

He turns to go before he has to see her reaction.

The good thing about hating being at home and being ashamed to go into school, Rose finds, is that she can spend the day with Aaron. It's like old times. Sometimes they walk down to the bridge, down through the woods. They sit in the hollow like they used to. They share a joint. Rose tells him about the places she's been.

'On the Tube, you have to stand, because there's too many people. You have to stand right pressed up against them. If you get off at Holborn, the escalators are the longest. You're on them for about five minutes. When you look down, the bottom of the escalator is tiny.

'If you get off at Covent Garden, there is only a lift, and everyone presses into it. You have to move forward to fill in all the gaps. Then when you get out, that's where all the shops are. There's all the big shops, and then all these others as well. They're all the clothes shops. It's like Silverways, only outside.

'If you go out, to a bar, there are drinks that cost twelve pounds each. At a restaurant, there are meals that cost hundreds. I had a meal, where there were two of us, and it came to two hundred pounds.'

'Is everyone rich?' says Aaron.

Rose nods. She knows what they would say. She asked Archie, and Titch. They both said they weren't. But she's seen their houses, and their clothes. She's seen the cupboard at the magazine, where new stuff is just chucked in a heap. She is learning, though. She's learning that they believe what they say.

'They don't say they are. They just look after you,' she says. 'They give you things. Anything you want.'

She remembers the feel of Titch's hand in hers.

She's going to London on Wednesday. She has another job. And she's decided, now, that once it's finished she won't go back to school, or to Graeme's.

'We're going to get a house,' she says. 'With a sofa.'

On Saturday, Graeme is away. Rose takes the L-plates off and drives down the narrow road that goes over the moor in her little car, with Aaron on the cushions at the back. She has the test on Tuesday. When she gets the licence, then they will be ready.

In the meantime, she loves driving. She puts the windows down. The air fills the little car.

They go slowly. The road is fringed with heather and bracken. The bracken is starting to wither and redden. The sky is blue, but streaked with thin trails of cloud, and the wind is fresh. The road dips sharply into a little gully, and the motor of the little car labours to climb out again the other side.

In the back seat Aaron is trying to skin up. The car jolts and the tobacco scatters.

'Can you stop?' he says.

Rose leans forward over the wheel. She peers through the windscreen. They pull into a grass layby.

They leave the car. They follow a path.

'Come on,' says Aaron.

Now they leave the path.

They walk across the moor. The heather is high and springy. When their feet brush over it, tiny insects rise, half-hearted, already dying as winter nears. Ahead of them is the rock, standing high, wind-carved.

Aaron walks ahead. The sun is warm, the wind cool. His legs are thin. He moves like a colt, ungainly, but with the promise of grace. Maybe he just needs more time, Rose thinks.

They approach the rock. Aaron stops, bends. Kneels. He has something in his shoe. Rose walks forward. Puts one hand to the warm stone. Rounds the corner. Stops.

Jack squats, grinning, in the sun-drenched nook.

Rose stands. He is wearing shorts and a grey T-shirt. His legs folded under him, his back arced forward as he rests on his heels. His calves are spattered with mud. His arms hang down in fluid ropes of muscle. A wet V of sweat is on his back, and his short hair is wet. His face is red, and his eyes wide and hungry with exertion.

Behind her, Aaron draws in.

'Smoke?' he says.

. . .

The three of them sit in the shelter of the rock. Aaron skins up. Rose sits in the middle. Jack has rolled back from his haunches and rests his back against the stone.

Rose can smell the peat, the stone, the sweat drying on Jack. His knee touches her leg. She moves.

He smiles. His eyes stay hard and hungry.

'How's London?' he says.

She shrugs.

'I bet you tell him more than that.'

She shrugs.

The moor dips towards the valley ahead of them. You can see the green scar of the treetops. Beyond it, moorland rolls on.

'How's Graeme?'

His eyes gleam.

'Still perving?'

She says nothing.

'Yes,' says Aaron.

'Don't blame him,' says Jack.

Aaron finishes the joint. He lights it. The paper crackles, and the thick smoke wafts across the three of them. He passes it to Rose. She draws on it. She holds the smoke inside her. The warmth of it rises inside her. She leans back. The sun is warm. The smoke drifts up from her open mouth.

She closes her eyes for a second. She feels the sun on her eyelids.

She passes the joint to Jack. She watches him inhale, then she looks back out to the moor, and the valley. It seems to her that this might be the last time she is here. She hasn't said it to anyone yet. But it is over. The last ties are cut – Dillon cut them. She has escaped.

She swallows the thin clear air. In the distance a tiny car beetles along a narrow ribbon of road over the moor. The damp of the old house sits in her nostrils.

She won't go back.

The thought sets off a complicated ache inside her for Aaron. He will come too – she has the story in her head. He will come and live with her. But he is also Aaron.

When he was small, he was so small. When he was five, he looked like a three-year-old. When he was seven, the year before they went to Graeme's house, he broke his arm. A friend of her mother's grabbed him by the arm and shook him, and it broke.

He's tall, now. He eats like he's making up for all he missed out on. But he's still brittle.

Jack reaches across her. She smells the rich stink of his armpit. He passes the joint back to Aaron.

Rose feels the rock behind her. The smooth curve, the gritty texture. Aaron on one side, Jack on the other. She won't do this again, and she's glad, but she's also sad for them. For all of them. She remembers the day she saw her mother in a doorway in Manchester, on a school trip. She was asleep, and she'd soiled herself.

The weak sunlight warms her face. The weed is good. But it makes her ache. Sometimes calm is painful. You slow down, and you have to look at things full on.

'So you're going to forget all about us,' says Jack.

His eyes have a warmth to them that Rose remembers. They used to sit in her room, looking at the pictures on her wall. Looking at the houses, and the figurines, and the clothes.

'No.'

No, she won't. Because he's her brother too. She's heard him cry at night.

'You will.'

His voice is flat. A statement.

She can feel the lack in him. He is missing something wonderful, something that makes us whole, and he knows it. She had Aaron. He had no one.

The sun glints on the edge of a cloud and the air chills. She reaches out to take his hand. At first he lets her. It's rough. It feels like the hand of someone twice his age. There is no softness anywhere, not even when her fingers reach round into the palm.

She can hear his breathing slow. The weed spreads inside her. She feels him, hardened into wood, a root grown tight in knots, coiled over itself, swirling loops of frozen grain clenched around some deep-buried sin. His black eyes squint into the sun. They glisten in the light. Briefly his hand closes over hers.

Then he flinches and draws it away. Before she can speak, he's pushed himself forward again, back onto his haunches, his body tense with movement.

'I heard your mum's on special offer.'

His lip has pulled back from his mouth. His teeth are yellow.

'Two holes for the price of one.'

He grins fully now, his mouth wide and delighted. He stands up. He moves with barely suppressed energy. He kicks his feet out one by one, like he's limbering up.

His eyes flick towards Aaron, leaning slack against the rock. Jack's head bobs and sways, but his eyes stay fixed on Aaron.

'Show us your tits,' he says to Rose. His damp T-shirt drifts in the wind, pulling at the hard lines of his chest. 'I haven't seen them for years.'

'Piss off,' says Rose. She stands too.

He carries on staring at Aaron while he talks. His voice has harrowed to a vicious point. 'I reckon little brother wants to see them too.'

Aaron sits, staring up. His eyes are big. His face has that twist to it, like someone's pulling at the skin from inside. She knows he will never be OK. Even if he lives with her in a cottage with roses and smoke coming out of the chimney, he will never be OK.

Nor will Jack, and nor will she.

She turns to walk off. She raises her legs high to step over the heather. The dust of the dying year rises from it.

'Fucking pricktease.'

She hears a noise behind her. Jack is there, eyes tight, mouth clenched in a thin dark slit. He reaches as she turns and grabs her hair and pulls. Her head jerks back, and she stumbles, and then he is on her and his knee strikes between her legs and his weight is on her and his face is inches from hers, narrow, bullet hard, rage filled.

And then with a thud his head snaps to one side and he falls away from her.

She scrambles back. Her legs are still entangled with his. They are heavy, immobile. The heather scrapes against her neck, and where her T-shirt has ridden up her back. Aaron is standing, still, looking down at the two of them. He has a rock about the size of a brick in one hand.

She closes her eyes. For one second, she lies, in the dark,

in the heather. She smells the peat, the moss. She smells the grass, dry and rich. She smells Jack, the sweat of him, and a sharper, more subtle smell. An old smell, older than the moors and the forest and the rocks.

Then she sits up. Aaron's trembling, but he smiles at her. After all, this isn't the worst thing that's ever happened to them.

'Again?' says Andy.

'She's your sister,' replies Paula.

Titch is coming next weekend. Last minute. She has an idea, she says. About Rose.

Andy and Paula are sitting at the front of their house. Paula is in her running gear, ready to go. She drinks a glass of water, he drinks a beer. The colours of the trees are turning, drifting into brittle browns and yellows, cooling and hardening. The air is sharp, but the garden is a suntrap. Andy's hair is too long, flying high in odd strands above his thinning scalp. His face is pleasingly lined, narrow eyed. Paula feels the stirrings of desire. In recent years, it has been intermittent, but fierce when it comes. They have months without, then weeks with nothing but. It feels seasonal, timed to the pull of something neither of them can see.

Paula really doesn't want Titch around.

They last saw her three weeks ago. They visited her in London. When they arrived, the girl was there.

'Don't worry,' smiled Titch. 'Rose is leaving soon.'

Rose was on the sofa. Sprawled out like she was relaxing, but Paula had seldom seen anyone look less relaxed. She didn't know Rose well, yet had seen her daily for years. She had seen her as that stick-thin year seven in red glittery heels, and then as the withdrawn teen who walked around like the world didn't exist. She'd seen Rose, or at least the shape of Rose, hidden behind a curtain of hair at a PEP meeting, while her social worker and her carer spoke for her. And she'd spoken to her last year, when she started sixth form, when the two of them caught five minutes on the first day.

Looking at Rose, on Titch's sofa, Paula had such a vivid memory of that conversation. They ducked into an empty room to talk. Rose said very little. But she met Paula's eyes. She smiled, and she held her head straight and looked at Paula. Her face was greasy, but clear, neither childlike nor adult. Her smile came and went easily, underwritten by a kind of nervous carelessness, like she wasn't aware of how it looked, or that it could be seen at all.

'I'm so happy you've come back for sixth form,' Paula had said. 'You let me know if there is anything we can do.'

Rose's smile had lodged in Paula's mind that day, and she couldn't shake it. She looked at Rose on Titch's sofa. Her hair washed and cut, her legs long and frozen with awkwardness.

Later, when she had gone to catch her train, Paula took Titch to one side.

'I don't think you know what you are doing.'

Titch looked pained.

'I don't mean it isn't good.' Paula hesitated. She had no idea what she really wanted to say, let alone how to say it. But she was also certain she would say it. For all of her care, and professionalism, there was a little imp of envy inside her that Titch might have encroached on her world and by accident done something amazing. 'I just mean these things are really delicate.'

'What things?'

'That girl.' She hesitated again, and then she was on surer ground. She found what it was her mind had been circling round since she saw Rose. 'She has no foreground. She has nothing to give her a sense of scale or perspective.' Was that it? 'And you have to be careful about yourself, too.' That might be it. 'You are putting yourself – and me – in a really odd position.'

Titch was annoyed. Paula knew she only heard the last sentence. 'You needn't worry. We're taking good care of her.'

They had moved on. They stayed the rest of the weekend, and Rose wasn't mentioned. But Paula knew the dynamic between them had shifted, and might shift further. On the train home, as the fields ticked past, she'd thought about Titch. About her hermetic little life. About the choices both of them had made and the thousand little failures they hid. She could see her sister-in-law, the warmth of her, and then, like the sun slipping behind a cloud, the chill.

The landscape deepened as they headed north. Forests rose and grew in front of her, and she felt the tangle of years around her heart.

'Paula?' says Andy.

In the garden, Paula blinks, smiles.

'Let's pretend we're away,' says Andy.

The thought of it is a cool hand on a hot brow. This is not how it needs to be. The autumn sun sends shafts of light through the dark trees. Maybe it might just all dissolve into nothing.

Paula leans forward, delicately poised. She puts a hand onto Andy's groin. He smiles at her. They head inside.

. . .

By the time she gets out on her run it's almost five. She has an hour of light, dimming towards dusk. She wears high vis, but even so, she'd rather go on the moors than the roads if she's running the risk of being caught out in the dark. She's less afraid of werewolves than of crap drivers. She has a tiny head torch in any case.

At her gate, Paula turns left. She runs fast. She feels the looseness of sex about her still, and the sweat starts quicker than she had expected in the cold air. She breathes in Andy with the mud of the track and the drying heather. It feels good that she can do this, have afternoon sex then go for a run. She'll drink wine later, and sleep deeply.

Fuck you, Titch, she thinks.

She catches herself. Then she smiles, her mouth open with exertion.

Fuck you, Titch, she thinks again.

The adrenaline pumps through her. She's running fast, a little too fast for herself, but she can do it.

She is not a phoney. She does things right. She will speak to Rose on Monday.

She's higher now, and the sun streams across the moors in sudden space. Her breath is ragged from the climb, but each gasp feels full and strong and flecked with curses.

Fuck you, Titch.

As she pulls over the lip of the hill and onto the slight downward dip her stride lengthens and loosens and her mouth gapes wider into almost a laugh at herself, a laugh if she wasn't pulling hard for every breath.

You fucking idiot, Paula, she thinks.

She will talk to Rose on Monday. She will. She will talk to

Rose on Monday, and say the things that no one is saying. That this is not real. That these people are not real. That this is glamour, enchantment, rats turned into pageboys and lizards masquerading as photographers.

Fuck you, Titch, she thinks.

In the sky, the sun hangs between banks of cloud. When it drifts behind, the chill of autumn sweeps across the moor, and the sweat prickles icily on Paula's back. She runs faster.

It's been a while since she's been up here at this time of day, at this time of year. There is a heaviness to the land and to the sky, but the wind spreads and shifts between them with the light, cold touch of unbroken miles. Her face hardens in effort, her brows low as she holds herself straight and limber.

She feels strong but the thoughts that pace through on the beats of her heels on the hard mud darken.

She will see Rose on Monday, but what will she say? She speaks to children every day. She tells them what they should do, how they should be to get along, how they should fit the shapes they're supposed to. But she doesn't know them.

She thinks of the teachers she had, and the well-meaning things they said. To be a teacher means on some level being the voice of the norm, the voice of conformity. It means advising people to play the odds, to get the results, to behave. Those teachers wanted the best for her, but when they said 'the best', what they really meant was the average.

Andy would tell her that she's not like that, not like the teachers she had, who were old, and blind. That she cares, and thinks about what she does.

But Paula knows better. She knows that imperceptibly she has become old too. And she knows how difficult it is to tell the truth, because the truth is so slippery, and so painful. Most days it's easier to pretend that following the rules is the best thing for you, and if you do, it will all work out in the end.

She has a speech she gives, on resilience. She says how really, there's no wisdom that she can impart beyond simply saying don't stop. All you have to do is keep going, keep taking the knocks. No shortcuts. She believes what she says, and she knows it is what they need to hear. But she also feels the delicate equivocation of hard-won experience becoming brittle and glib as she puts it into words.

Fuck you, Paula, she thinks.

She runs her hand over her face, pulling the sweat from her eyes.

The light is failing. The sky darkens above her, but light still echoes up around the rim of the horizon. Her feet pound along the track. She can feel the ache and spring in her knees, the balance of muscle and bone, the tight power of her deep breaths.

Ahead of her is a rocky outcrop, beyond which a rough track curls back towards town. She'll go that far and then turn back.

A bird calls, sharp and thin across the twilight.

Her mood lifts.

Every now and then it works. You have that conversation, and something in the way you say it sticks. Nothing different about what you say. No special insight. But a glance, an inflection, a moment, and they hear you. You read the currents, the flow of things, and at the right moment you say the right thing, and everything changes.

She will talk to Rose on Monday. And when they talk, it will lift, and everything will change.

She reaches the rock. She stops, doubles over to touch her toes. Hangs like that for a moment. She straightens, pulls one foot back behind her, then another. Feels the flex of muscle inside her. Touches her thigh to feel the hard strength of it. Shakes herself. Pulls out the head torch – it's not dark yet, but may be soon.

She puts it on now, because she may as well.

Slowly, she picks her pace back to a run. She looks down at her feet, at the rough path, and then glances back at the rock, and the beam of the torch in the dimming twilight catches something, a flicker of reflective material, up to the left of the path.

She frowns, looks again, sees a trainer abandoned in the heather. Runs two steps closer. Sees the trainer is on a foot.

The moor is a thunder of blood in her. She feels the roll of her heart. She stands.

She can see the shape of where he lies.

The cold seizes her, bitingly, at the back of her sweat-soaked neck. She steps forward. Half in the dim light of evening, and half in the yellow of her head torch, she sees Jack, on his side, his face staring up. He's dead. Something has struck the side of his temple with such force that the skull has caved in.

Rose drives, Aaron in the passenger seat. He holds her phone in his hands, following a route. They drive on smaller roads. She has never been on a motorway.

'Knock knock,' he says.

'Who's there?'

'Boo!'

'Boo who?'

'Don't be such a baby!' Aaron crows.

She can only spare him the slightest glance. She needs all her concentration for the road. But she has to look, has to check. His voice is just like it was, but the rest of him, no. He's grown.

'Can I smoke?' he says.

She shakes her head.

'Please?'

She shakes her head.

'Why you such a moody bitch?'

She frowns at the road.

'Sorry,' he says. And then, 'Do you remember when we drove to the lake?'

She remembers. A friend of their mother's took them – Aaron was six, and she was nine. The lake had picnic tables beside it. On the way, they listened to the radio, and they sang along to 'American Boy'. The shore of the lake was a thin pebbled strip, and you could see a mountain on the other side. They had a stone-throwing competition. They watched other kids go in the water, but they didn't have costumes, so they rolled up their trousers and stood in the water. Their mother's friend – they were never told his name – brought a picnic. He had Hula Hoop crisps and ham sandwiches and bananas and digestive biscuits.

'Do you remember the biscuits?' says Aaron.

'Yes,' says Rose. She remembers the way her mother's friend looked at them while they ate.

The road winds along a river valley. Trees arc over. Houses cluster in groups along the sides of the road then melt away. They pass through a town. The town disappears again.

'You've not got enough battery.'

They need a charger and they need petrol. Rose has twenty pounds.

They stop at a petrol station. Rose goes in to check about the charger. It costs £5.99. She goes back to the pump and puts in just under fourteen pounds' worth. She is left with six pence.

The man serving is old, with spiky white and black peppered hair and a face that is lined and sagging. He looks at Rose, his watery eyes flicking across her, back and forth.

She smiles. She finds it hard sometimes to see whether people feel sorry for her or want to fuck her.

'What about Jack?' says Aaron.

There didn't seem much point in hiding him. She doesn't know what will happen when he's found. If he's found. Maybe they would think it was an accident.

She knows they won't think it was an accident.

The only thing she knows for certain now is that Aaron will not be OK. The thought is a thrum of anxiety at the back of her mind.

She knows this will end badly. But for the moment, she keeps driving.

The journey should take four hours. But they skip the motorway, so it should take seven. But they get lost, so when it gets dark, and Rose starts to panic because she's never driven at night, she pulls into a layby and they sleep in the car.

The autumn night is cold. They try the front two seats first, then they curl around each other on the back seat, like they used to.

At midnight, Rose is awake. Aaron is sleeping. His limbs lie slack and heavy. His head rests on her arm, but her head tilts back to look out of the window. The shape of it is unfamiliar from this angle. Through it she can see trees, and beyond, stars. A car passes, near enough to hear, but far enough to provide no light.

She closes her eyes.

In dreams, she still holds Aaron. She feels him in her arms, but she cannot see him.

She wakes again. It's still dark. The air sits in cool pockets by her neck, chilled by the metal of the car door. Her stomach aches with hunger. She remembers a shoot. She dreams it. She sits at a table, long and elegant and fake. Fifteen burgers are used. All of them are cold. They have neat semicircles bitten out of them. They have tampons soaked in boiling water buried in them. Steam rises appetisingly.

Archie is there. She kisses him. He pulls her towards him. She kisses him and now they are in his flat, like they were, exactly like they were. She is remembering, but she is dreaming. In the dream, she is taller, stronger. They are in his flat, and the diamond-patterned wallpaper is peeling, and the stairs are littered with broken things. She tastes him. She kisses him and she bites his lip. She wraps her legs around him and she squeezes. His face is white and scared.

She wakes again. The car is filled with misty grey light. The window is covered with condensation. Her arm is numb under the bony weight of Aaron's head, and her shoulder aches. She shifts slightly, raising herself up. Aaron's head tips gently to one side. She looks at him, checking to see he's still sleeping. His eyelids are blue. She can see his eyeballs moving beneath them.

She reaches up and wipes away the moisture from the window with her hand. She raises her head too until she can peer over the edge of the window. The grassy verge sparkles with dew. She presses her forehead to the cold window, her lips and nose touching the plastic of the door. She can see her hairline in the wing mirror. She lifts her head farther, craning her neck. She can see her eye.

Aaron stirs and blinks, and Rose moves sharply, released.

They step out of the car. They stretch, stiff. Their bodies are lean and chill easily in the raw air. Rose smiles at the dirt on Aaron's face. She looks in the wing mirror properly now. Her face is grey, her hair wild, her eyes bright with hunger.

She looks back at Aaron and laughs. He grins delightedly.

A shiver runs up her back. It touches her spine delicately, sharply, and as she tries to throw it from her with a movement of her shoulders, she knows that in seconds she will be undone. The heat of love is bright and painful, and she cannot bear it.

But then Aaron steps in to her, and she squeezes him in a fierce hug, and she presses her nose into the sour skin of his neck.

Sunday. They drive again, following the winding roads.

The landscape is gentler here. The roads wind between high hedges. Rose drives slowly. Cars come fast, and you have to creep past each other, twigs rattling against the side of the car. They pass through a village.

'The stone is a different colour,' says Aaron.

The stone is yellow. It seems the wrong colour for stone.
The church looks wrong too. And the fence.
They pass through.

'Do you remember the first house,' Rose says.
Aaron nods.
'You were only three.'
'You told me.'
'But do you remember?'
He shakes his head. 'But you told me about the wallpaper.'

The roads here twist, warren-like. The car tunnels through the landscape. At another town they pull up beside a bus stop. An old lady sits with a bag on wheels and a stick.

She seems unaware of them. She looks to one side, to where the bus will come from. Her face is ruckled and blinking.

'Excuse me,' says Rose quietly.

The old lady stares resolutely towards the bus that hasn't come.

Rose puts the car into gear and moves off.

The car windows are open. The air is cold. Rose wishes Aaron would remember. That was the house where they had a sofa, before her nan died. She remembers sitting on the stairs, looking at the diamond-patterned wallpaper, the sun passing through the small window in the front door and laying a different diamond, bright and warm, across the pattern. She thinks she remembers it. But she also remembers quiet nights on those same stairs, the door frame empty, the dark, the damp cold air and Dillon beside her.

'I remember breaking the house,' says Aaron.

He has a dreamy expression.

'That was amazing.'

The road unspools in front of her, between endless hedges. Yes, it was. The day they did it was amazing. Their mother took them at night. She was ten and Aaron was seven. Their mother had seen the door was broken. When they went in, Rose thought they were going to stay. The house had been empty since they left. Their crockery was still in the cupboards, and their list of important numbers was still taped to the inside of the cutlery drawer. The people who'd broken in had left drifts of cider bottles. Their mother looked around. Then she handed Rose a plate, and Aaron a plate, and she took one herself.

'Ready?' she said.

Rose didn't know what they were ready for. Then her mother yelled, 'Go,' and hurled the plate at the wall so hard it smashed into what must have been a thousand pieces.

They broke everything they could. It was amazing. But afterwards, Rose felt an emptiness inside her, hard and strangely solid, like she was hungrier than she had ever been before, but was too full to eat.

They follow the road, between the hedges. She is tired. The road curls. She feels like she is travelling in circles.

She remembers the house. The dark. Dillon, on the stairs. If she closes her eyes she can hear him.

'Rose!'

The car swerves. Sticks clatter against the wing mirror, then she's up on the other bank and then down again with a bump. The engine cuts out.

Aaron grins, excitedly.

'Sorry.'

The engine starts again, and they curl on, between hedges. Her hands grip tight on the wheel. They turn a corner, and roll to a slow stop.

They are here.

The wooden gate is set in a low brick wall. The garden is small, trim, lined with busy clipped box hedges and a tiny twisting paved path. Roses climb the whitewashed walls, hanging low over a bench, and beside it, a birdbath. The roof is a smooth curve of perfect thatch over twinkling black timber-framed windows, capped with a squat chimney.

Behind the wheel of the car, Rose closes her eyes. She breathes deeply. In her pocket she fingers the hard shapes of the key she took from Titch's kitchen two weeks ago.

Aaron gazes in awe. It seems like a house from a dream, not one that you might go into. It is a house from a book, from a fairy tale.

He expects dwarves. Or bears. Or best of all, gingerbread.

The smell is what strikes them first. You might expect a house like this to smell damp, and old, but there is a rich vanilla scent that greets them. The porch is dark, but they see curling leaves covering the walls. They find the light. The leaves are filled with birds, bright parrots perching in the wallpapered foliage.

And on. Through the next door. A hall, a mirror, a light hanging down in green glass. Stairs rising up. Cream carpets, rich and full. Another door, a living room, huge, extending back into a bright white kitchen under the glass of an extension. They walk through. The light is golden. Beyond the extension they see a garden, stretching back in parallel stripes, borders heavy with hanging leaves. In the centre of the lawn is a perfect circle of earth, and an apple tree grows out of it. All around the base are scattered apples, left to rot.

The wide space of the extension is filled with a long table made of a rich, red wood. A lamp hangs over it, suspended on a curved sliver of metal. In the opposite corner is a wood-burning stove, and a deep cream sofa.

For a moment, they stand still in the scented air. Then Aaron turns to Rose. His lopsided face, pulled tight with worry, eases into a wide smile. His hair sticks up in loose, greasy spikes. His skin is clouded with grime. But he is young. When he smiles, he is young.

Rose smiles back.

'Can we eat?' he says.

The kitchen is behind them. There are rows and rows of cupboards. She cautiously opens one. Bowls. Two stacks of ten each. She takes one out. It seems whiter than a normal bowl. She puts it back.

Then mugs. Fifteen mugs, all identical, all upside down. Cups too, with saucers. Then glasses, dozens of them. Different shapes, stacked in different areas. Big wide-bottomed goblets. Narrow flutes. Artisan water glasses. Then big bowls. Serving bowls. Blue, white, terracotta, with seagulls flying across them or fish swimming at the bottom. Plates, stacked twenty high, in three different sizes.

Then jam. Nine different half-opened jars of jam.

She pulls out strawberry, hands it to Aaron. She takes blackberry. He dips a finger in, hooks a strawberry, eats. She does the same then holds the jam in one hand as she opens drawers, finds a spoon. She gives him one and he switches to that, spooning the jam into his mouth.

The sweetness fills her.

She moves on. The lower cupboards have pans in. She checks them. More pans. Trays. Food mixers. Tea and coffee.

There is a door at the back of the kitchen. She opens it. Behind her Aaron is still spooning jam. A light clicks on.

From floor to ceiling are shelves of food.

Cans, packets, bottles. Wine, beer, oil. Boxes of cereal, six-packs of drinks cans.

Biscuits.

She steps into the cupboard. She looks back. Aaron has jam on his face, in the corners of his mouth. He looks like a toddler.

Let this work, she thinks to herself. Let us stay here, alone. Let us eat.

The sweetness of the jam has opened a deep, aching hole that cramps inside her. She hasn't eaten for twenty-four hours. She hasn't felt like this for years. She might faint, crumple onto the floor and disappear.

That Monday morning, seven years before, she had walked to school slowly. She placed her feet gently, carefully, in her bright red shoes, the ones her mother had stolen for her. She had already dropped Aaron at primary. In their room at the hostel, when they left that morning, her mother had still not returned. She had been gone since Friday night. Rose had bought a pack of biscuits on the way home from school on Friday afternoon. They finished them for breakfast on Sunday.

When their mother wasn't there, Aaron refused to leave the room. He was scared of the hallway, and the people in the hallway. Rose couldn't leave him either. If she did he screamed. So they peed in a bucket and poured it out of the window when the coast was clear. If there was a pigeon, they tried to hit it. Once, they got a cat.

She had found that if you walk slowly, you get less dizzy.

At school, she had waited, on the bench, far from the others. She had looked at her feet, red and strange at the end of her legs, and thought of the mad dash down the street, her mother shouting at her to run. She tried to taste again the fizzing cola bottle. She had already checked the bins, but it was Monday morning, and there was nothing to eat in them. She remembers the way the bell rang through her, jangling her teeth. When you're hungry, the world is either distant or too close. People are ghosts, until they come close, and then their voices pierce you like knives. She waited a moment, as the noise eddied around her. She blinked against it, all these bodies, thick and strong and full of life. She walked to the door of the classroom and then they saw her shoes.

The edge of the door is hard behind her back. The jar is cold in her hand.

They took her to the head teacher. In the corner of the window of Mrs Jackson's office there had been a small crack like a crooked smile. Rose had stared at it so she didn't have to look at the plate of custard creams on the desk. She stared until it stared back. The eyes were narrow flecks of paint. It looked like her mother.

Remember me? it said, squinting.

Rose had wobbled for a moment on her heels. One hand reached out, slowly, and her pale fingers touched the edge of the desk to steady herself.

'Rose?' said Mrs Jackson.

She had tried to look away, but the wicked little eyes held her.

Remember they're all bitches, Rose. The crack grinned, lop-sided. *Wizened little cunts. Fat fucking liars, all of them.*

'Rose!' said Mrs Jackson.

Mrs Jackson's voice was sharp. Rose tore her eyes away and stared, blinking, at the head teacher. She was tall and narrow and tightly bound in a suit and jacket. Her face was hard, witchy, polished at the high cheekbones and on the ridge of the long nose. A glint of light caught the tip of it.

'Would you like a biscuit?' said Mrs Jackson.

It felt like a test.

The head teacher's eyes had given nothing away. Rose had looked down at the plate, trying to figure out the answer. There were so many custard creams that they were piled on top of each other. After a moment, Mrs Jackson had pushed the plate gently towards her fingers.

'Take one,' she had said.

The edge of the door is hard behind her back. The jar is cold in her hand.

Sometimes it seems to Rose that everything is a test. The world is run by rules no one has told her. They haven't even told her what they haven't told her.

And right now she is so hungry she can't think straight.

Maybe it might happen again. She might faint, and wake up, and Mrs Jackson will lie her on the sofa in the office and feed her custard creams and they will give her a house.

This house.

. . .

The front door clicks open.

Titch doesn't know why she goes to church. It's part of her routine here. She would never go in London. When she's here, it just seems right. The church is a hundred yards away, and as you walk through the wooden gate, through the old part of the graveyard, where the stones lean, mossy and worn, and in at the damp porch where old notices moulder on the corkboard and the flagstones have the faint tracings of someone's life and death, you are part of something very English. It is worth preserving, she thinks.

When she drives through the new housing estate, with its neat narrow geometric blocks, its clean brick, its forest of black-tiled roofs, she feels a sadness inside for a gentler past, one with fewer sharp edges.

She feels old, sometimes. She works with young people, and although she's not old – not yet – it can seem like she's slowly fading from view. She is slower than they are. She looks sometimes at them, at Rachael and Jacqui, at Archie, and she is amazed by how much they want, and how quickly. When she was their age, she couldn't begin to afford some of the designers they wear. She drove an old banger, not a cute little Mini on lease.

Rose is different, of course. Rose seems to glide through things, not wanting, just accepting. She has a wonderful calm to her. Titch wonders whether going through what she has been through has made her more grateful, more willing to just be in the moment, without grasping all the time for the main chance.

It's that grasping quality she really hates. She knows she's not free of it herself, and that her magazine has a role in stoking that acquisitiveness. But maybe there's still time for a rethink. Sometimes the world seems so fast, and so cruel. All the bulletins every night on the news, the inequality, the rapaciousness – and underneath, the ominous drumbeat of climate change. Surely we can't just carry on having more stuff, more people, more growth? Every day it seems more of an effort to persuade herself that things are going to be OK.

And then she leaves London and she feels, here, with the smell of hay in the air, and the lush hedgerows, and the sense of layers of history held together by a community, that there might be a better way to live. An ordinary, everyday kind of life. Sustainable.

In the churchyard, she wonders sometimes about just retreating. Leaving them to fight it out, and living out here, simply, quietly. Spending her time doing good things – small, good things. Eating organic. She doesn't need much, she thinks. She doesn't need holidays, or Michelin-starred meals, or film premieres.

Just her little cottage.

The roses give a faint scent as she walks up the path. Flowers. If you could have a garden, that might be enough. She imagines herself, an old lady on her lawn, daisies at her feet.

She turns the key. She walks through the hall, and into the living room.

She sees Aaron first. He stands between the kitchen and the sofa. He's wearing a grey tracksuit, muddy and sagging at the knees. His trainers are black, his socks are grey school socks. He's tall, skinny, dirty. He has jam on his face, and is spooning it out of a jar. He looks at her, spoon in hand. His eyes are raw, and his mouth slack. He looks like some kind of goblin.

She freezes. Then, when he does nothing, she says, quietly, 'What are you doing?'

Aaron turns towards his sister. She steps out from the kitchen.

'Oh,' says Titch.

Rose looks at her. Titch looks back.

Rose wants to smile, but the smile won't come. So she stares. She stares at Titch's careful makeup, her lined face, the smooth, neat ugliness of her clothes. And Titch stares back at the coiled, dirty beauty of Rose.

The two of them stare for so long that suddenly Rose wonders if Titch doesn't recognise her.

'It's Rose,' says Rose.

She waits, uncertain now if Titch has even heard her.

'I know,' Titch says, eventually. She looks back at Aaron, and opens her mouth to say something. Instead she looks again at Rose. 'How did you get in?'

'We drove,' says Rose.

The three of them stand, watching each other. The sun is bright through the skylight of the extension. It falls in a fierce white block across the table. The room is big, Rose thinks. Titch seems far away from her, like they're outside, or in the foyer of her office. She turns to look behind her, scanning the room, her long coat swaying above her trim ankles.

Rose knows she has to say this right. 'We thought we could stay.'

Titch turns back. She looks at Rose intently, with a slight frown. 'Yes, but how did you get in?'

Rose hesitates. She is blind, tapping her way through. There is a route, she knows, she just has to stay calm and take it slowly.

'You said you never get out here,' she says.

Titch says, 'I asked you a question.'

Her voice is hard. The room chills.

Rose feels her pulse begin to race. She cannot take it slowly now. She has to say it. She tries to think of the thing to say. She feels the words tripping away from her. In her head it is clear. There has to be a way of saying it – that she needed to come here. She needed it. More than she needed a dress, or a lipstick, or to suck Archie's cock in the toilets of a posh restaurant.

'I took the key,' she says.

Titch's face is impassive.

This feels like falling. It always feels like falling. She knows she is falling. But there is magic here, surely. There is magic that will catch her, and lift her up, her and Aaron, and set them safe.

The white light burns across the smooth table. Titch's heel clicks sharp as she shifts her foot back, shifts her weight on her hips.

Rose moves too, enough for the sun to flare on the clear glass.

We will never be safe, she thinks.

'Where from?' asks Titch.

Titch is still standing on the same spot, still half on the turn, weight on one hip. She is still holding her handbag.

'Your flat,' says Rose, quietly.

'Get out.'

Aaron looks at Rose. His face is pale beneath the grime.

'Get out!'

Rose looks back. At Aaron, at Titch. At the immaculate white sofa. She is still holding the blackberry jam in one hand, the spoon in the other.

The thing that grips her is tight beneath her jaw. It's pissing in a bucket. Picking sandwiches from a bin. Men's eyes, men's fingers. It's Aaron, and watching Aaron sink. It's being invisible, and then being stared at. It's voices, adult voices, picking her up and telling her things will be all right, and they never are.

Ever.

Fuck you, she thinks. *Fuck all of you.*

She digs the spoon into the jar. She pulls it out. Titch watches her. Then she flicks the spoon, and a dollop of jam sails across the room onto the sofa.

Aaron claps his hand to his mouth in glee.

Titch's jaw drops.

The jam has drawn a purple-black spatter along the floor and onto the arm of the sofa.

The three of them wait, on the cusp of something. Rose is light headed. She smiles. Aaron smiles at her.

She has wings. She can step up and dance on the air. She is nothing.

'I'm calling the police,' says Titch.

Aaron turns and, like a baseball pitcher, hurls his jar as hard as he can against the wall. It bursts with a sticky thunk.

Titch flinches and raises her hands to her head. She lets out a little shriek. She scrabbles for her phone. Rose steps forward and knocks it out of her hand. It skitters along the floor.

Aaron howls like a dog.

In the garden, a magpie hops across the lawn. The grass is damp, neat. Its tail bounces up and down. It dances between apples, lying rotting in the warm autumn sun. Its eye is a shiny black pebble, a hard, bright hole.

Rose takes Titch by the hair. She pulls her to the larder door. She slams the door on her head until the blood runs on the terracotta tiles. And when she's finished, they break the house.

Will Bradman has come into school with his union representative. He waits at reception. Paula's secretary ushers him into the office.

Paula tries to mask her shock.

Will's large, hearty body occupies a similar space, but the shape of it is newly angular. His face is pale, and his eyes glisten. When she looks up again, his gaze is fixed on her still.

'He had left school for almost a year before anything happened. He was twenty,' he says, in careful tones.

Paula nods.

'I am not a pervert.'

At the last word his composure cracks, and a fleck of spit comes from his mouth.

'I know, Will.'

He looks at her, and she forces herself to meet his gaze.

'This is not prosecutable,' she says. 'It is not a police matter. But there are legitimate concerns about conduct at play here. We will have to write you a letter of management advice, based on our discussions here, warning you about inappropriate contact with students.'

'A hug,' says Will firmly.

Paula carries on. 'And about the importance of separating your professional life from your personal life.'

The rep gives him a glance and Will says nothing.

'This letter will be on file.'

Will listens to the rest in silence.

He returns to work. On the first day, Paula sees him sitting in his car in the carpark and crying, huge heaving sobs that make his broad shoulders shake.

They might have escaped. They might have carried on running. Rose could have driven them to a Channel port, and gone to France. She might have dyed her hair, worn a long trench coat and dark glasses. Aaron could have worn a wig.

Imagine them on the deck of a ferry, Rose's hair whipping around her face. Aaron grinning in delight. He looks looser, happier. The kinks have been ironed out. He holds himself more like a real boy and less like a broken puppet. Rose smiles too. She has rescued him, from the wolves and the witches and the fairy godmother.

But they didn't go to France. They had no passports. They had never needed them. London was the farthest Rose had ever been.

They didn't even leave the house. After they had thrown the plates, and smashed the glasses, and opened every tin and box they could, and hurled the eggs at the window, and drunk the milk until it poured from the corners of their mouths, they curled up together on the jam-stained sofa and went to sleep.

Titch was the first to wake up. She found herself, bloodied, on her kitchen floor. At the hearing you could still see the mark of the door on her, a long straight scar surrounded by fading yellow bruises at her temple. She called the police, and when they came, Rose and Aaron were still asleep. They shook them, pulled them up, but they clung to sleep with a fierce tenacity. Eventually, the police waited beside them while the ambulance crew took Titch, and the officers began to catalogue the scene.

Still they slept.

In all the din of the crime scene, the radios, the flash photography, they lay on the sofa. Finally, the officers carefully prised them apart, and held them upright until their eyes blinked open.

Only when they took Aaron away did Rose react. It took three officers to hold her.

In court her face was still bloodied and swollen. One officer's elbow had caught her on the bridge of her nose, and her eyes glinted fiercely behind broad black bruises. She had blood crusted across her lip. She smiled throughout, a gleeful smile, free and feral, like she'd never been so happy.

After the hearing those who had watched and testified stand around in the lobby of the courtroom. Graeme approaches Titch. Her wet eyes are dimmed with fear and a kind of shame.

'I'm sorry,' he says.

She makes a gesture, faint.

Paula is at her head-teacherly best, tailored into narrow precision. 'Hi, Graeme,' she says.

It's funny, he thinks, but you forget these things. You forget that Paula Jackson was once Paula Mason, who used to wear charity shop tracksuits, and that before she lived in that posh house on the hill she was two doors down. Graeme sees her every now and then, in school, around. They've even had meetings about Rose. But he never really talks to her, not as a friend, or someone he once shared a joint with.

'Hi, Mrs Jackson,' he says.

He tells this to Caz on the way home.

'I can't believe you ever got stoned with Mrs Jackson,' she says.

'Claim to fame,' he says. He remembers the arch of the bridge, and Ash. Paula Mason, sitting with the rest of them, skinny and boyish and determined to be cool, if only for that one summer.

Was it as simple as that? That Paula wasn't attractive enough, and so she got away? That Ash was beautiful, and doomed?

'I tried to speak to Rose, you know,' he says.

'About what?'

The road sweeps between high pine forests.

'About how she needed to be careful.'

The thick dark trees flicker as they pass.

'Of what?'

He doesn't quite notice the ice in her voice.

'The way they made her look. In those photos.'

The road climbs. The trees fall away. The moors rise around them, long and quiet and dim in the dusk. There are few cars, and the radio is off. The hum of the motor and the zip of the tyres on the road are all they hear.

'I do feel bad,' he says, after a while.

The words catch in his throat. He doesn't know who they are for, Ash, or Rose, or Caz. He knows he's done nothing wrong, but he can't help feeling guilty.

It's dark by the time they get back. He drops Caz at her house. She doesn't touch him as he says goodbye. Just as she's going she stops and turns.

'You know, it's not what someone looks like. It's how they're looked at.'

She never says that it's over, but she doesn't call.

They put Aaron in juvenile detention. Rose goes to a normal prison, on a charge of GBH. She gets three years. Graeme asks to visit, but she says no. Aaron doesn't mind.

He goes as often as he can. Each time it is an effort, but he feels he owes it to the boy. And to Rose.

Aaron is pleased to see him. No one else visits. In a way, the place suits him. At least there are rules, straightforward rules you can learn and follow. There is no code to crack, no secret knowledge that will suddenly help you explain the relevance of sixteenth-century poetry, or Newtonian laws of physics, or glaciation.

But, for all the smiles, and the stilted chat about the food, Graeme can see there is something inescapable happening. Aaron is growing up, and with that comes a haunted look that settles around his eyes. He's always been damaged – there is nothing anyone can do to fix that. But it's heartbreaking to see him realise it.

He'll get out when he's twenty-one. It's easier not to think about what will happen to him then.

. . .

At home, Graeme takes down all the pictures. Rose using spot cream. Rose on a phone. Rose in trainers, Rose in a dress. Rose on the red carpet, twirling in the moment that everyone suddenly began to look at her.

There are no photos of Aaron.

At night, he sees Rose in his dreams, still. She's young, eleven, stick-thin, her uniform hanging from her like she's not even there. She looks at him, with those hungry eyes, and then he wakes, filled with disgust.

He wasn't the worst of them, he knows. But that's not enough.

Just before the final bell, on the last day of the autumn term, four days before Christmas, Paula's PA tells her that Dillon Caldwell wants to talk to her.

She knows what this will be about, and it makes her uncomfortable.

But it must be done. This is her job too.

'Hi, Dillon,' she says. He steps in. He's taller than she remembers. They are always taller than she remembers.

'Hi, Mrs Jackson.'

His hair is short. His Adam's apple is pronounced. He is thinner, leaner, more male than he was, and yet suddenly, strikingly, pretty.

Even a few months can do this. They walk differently. They bloom into the bone-sharp beauty of young adulthood.

She wants to smile, but she holds back. She's well used to being a teacher now, but still it can take you by surprise, how we get from there to here. There's no map. She's still not sure how she found her way.

Dillon's eyes dart uneasily around the room.

'Have a seat, Dillon.'

He sits.

'How can I help?'

Dillon casts his eyes down, then up at her. He looks directly at her.

'Mr Bradman said he's leaving.'

Paula nods. She waits. She needs to play her part.

'I don't think it's right.'

'It is his choice,' Paula says gently.

'But you made him leave.'

Dillon has a fierce look now. He is hunched forward. She can still see the little round-faced boy in him, but only just.

'You know we had to do that investigation,' she says.

Dillon shook his head. 'No, I don't. He gave me a hug. That's ridiculous.' He is speaking confidently now, angry, but in control. 'He was the teacher I knew best, and he saw I was struggling. My mum died, and it was difficult, and he was punished for helping me.'

Paula knows this boy will never forgive her, not if she talks about rules and conduct and safeguarding for the next hour.

'I'm sorry,' she says.

He frowns. She can see she hasn't soothed him. There is another betrayal in apologising, like she knows he's right, but she still won't change anything.

She tries again. 'Once something is out of the bag, it can't go back in. The whole school was talking about it. It would have been worse if we hadn't investigated.'

His face clouds. Up until now he has seemed almost a man. But the boy in him breaks through.

'It's not fair.'

The sharpness of the pain takes Paula by surprise. The echo of another boy, lip out, protesting at life. She concentrates on Dillon. The room is a little smaller, and he is a little closer.

She begins to speak, but then catches herself. Outside, a whistle blows and a bell rings. A noise swells in the building, doors bang, and she can hear the shouts of kids as they leave for the holidays. They rise and echo between the high walls of the school buildings, joyful and angry, wild and innocent, loud, crackling with energy.

Paula holds herself carefully. She is high up, balancing on something. She waits, and Dillon waits. Then she steps forward into the pain, because she always does.

'I had a conversation, once.' She swallows. 'I said something similar.' She hesitates again. She senses the space beneath her, the great empty void of freedom.

'I was talking to my mother.'

He looks at her, surprised.

'I asked her why it should be fair that a particular thing would happen.'

She finds the memory, a smoothed stone of hard-won comfort that she has held tight in her fist for many years.

'I asked her why it should be that my life would have this . . . gap.' She pauses. Her mother's hands were paper skinned. They sat in her lap, curled, thick knuckled. When she held them, the fingers moved around hers with stiff tenderness.

'She was quite old.'

She died soon after.

'She said that she didn't know anyone who didn't have a gap in their lives.'

Paula's mouth turns up wryly at one side, an unexpectedly mischievous movement.

'She was pretty blunt, my mum. What she actually said was she didn't know anyone who didn't have a gaping fucking hole in their life.'

Dillon is looking at her in astonishment. She smiles fully at him, now, a warm smile. Her angular face slips with surprising ease into kindliness. 'What she meant was just that sooner or later we all lose something. And we go through life hungry to fill the space it left.'

I'm sorry it happened so soon, for you, she thinks.

'We can't regain what we lose. We never stop being hungry. But we can find something else that might take the edge off it.'

His face is pale and alert.

Outside, the shouts are already fading. Schools are places of aching sadness, Paula thinks. Sometimes she can't bear it.

She looks at Dillon. His anger is wavering. She catches a thought, the faintest of intuitions.

'You can't blame yourself, Dillon.' She feels the delicate touch of possibility. 'And you can't blame Rose either.'

At her name his pale cheeks flush a bright pink.

'People talk for all sorts of reasons. It's rarely malicious.' She pauses, carefully holding in her amusement. Maybe she can bear it a little longer. 'Sometimes people just want to impress their friends.'

As she drives home, Paula watches the white line in the middle tick away. She imagines veering slowly over. She imagines the crash.

She won't do it.

She thinks of Dillon. He's the age Finn would have been. She thinks of his broadening shoulders, his confident walk.

She'll run when she gets home.

In February, Alisha and Dillon decide that enough is enough, and they should just go out with each other. They kiss, and one night, round at Alisha's house when her parents are away, they get as far as Alisha reaching into Dillon's trousers. Only he flinches when she touches him, and then she catches his eye and collapses into giggles, and the experiment fails.

They get stoned instead, wrapped in blankets, smoking carefully out of the open window.

After some time, Alisha leans over to him.

'I wish I could go out with you.'

Dillon giggles. 'We just tried that.'

She shakes her head. 'I know. I just wish it worked.'

Dillon looks at her. He knows her so well now. He remembers when he watched her walk through the woods in front of him, and she seemed so exotic, untouchable. Now she's just his friend.

He tips his head back and groans theatrically.

'Hey,' she says. She pokes him.

'It's fucking depressing,' he says. His head is fogged. He's unsure whether he means it. But he does mean it. 'Girls say they like you, but as a friend, and what they mean is they don't want to fuck you.'

'Hey!' she says, louder. 'That was mutual, you prick!'

They settle into companionable silence.

'You don't, though, do you?' he says, after a while.

'What?'

'Want to fuck me.'

'No.'

The air is cold. Through the window, they can see the deep black shadows of the trees, and through their bare branches, stars.

Somehow it seems that anything is permissible, now.

'Do you miss Jack?' he asks.

'I'm not sorry to never see him again.' She seems like she's going to say something else, for a second, but no.

'What's the connection?'

'What do you mean?'

'Why are you asking about Jack?' Her eyes narrow.

Dillon shrugs. 'He never got stuck in the friendzone.'

Alisha lets out a long, slow breath. It lies somewhere between disappointment, exasperation and sadness.

They look out at the stars.

'Do you miss Rose?' asks Alisha, after a while.

Dillon thinks. It suddenly seems to him that he's spent a lot of time thinking about love, and sex, and desire, and who he wants, and when, and how much. And it seems like, 'Do you miss her?' is an easier question.

'Yes,' he says.

He thinks a little more.

'Every day,' he says.

AFTER

Many things will happen. Alisha and Dillon and the rest of their class will finish their A-levels. They will dance on the street in the June nights, singing their freedom. Then Alisha will return to school in September to resit, chastened.

Dillon will accept a place at university, but he won't go, not yet. He'll work for a while, building up some money. He'll make films in the woods, on his own, arty, pretentious films that one day he will be embarrassed of. Not yet, though. Now, in this pause before adulthood, he'll look through the camera at the path from the bridge, and the rocky hollow, and the low rich green of the forest floor, and know that he's the first person to have seen these things, and they are his.

One night he'll talk to his dad, properly, about his mum.

He'll meet Alisha at the school gates some days and walk to the bridge. They'll stand on the parapet, now, and smoke a cigarette together. Sometimes they'll see the younger kids under the arches, smell the weed drifting up, hear the shrieks and the laughter.

Sometimes, at night, he'll go and sit quietly on the stairs in the empty house at the end of the long block.

Sometimes he'll write letters. Sometimes he'll receive them.

And in May, while Alisha is doing her exams for the second time, Dillon will borrow his dad's car and drive down to an anonymous town with a new-build prison outside it. He will wait in the car until the doors open, and Rose emerges. He will just look, at first.

She won't be the same, now. Her body will be leaner, stronger, clad in grey tracksuit. Her face will be blunter, her nose still squint from the policeman's elbow. Her hair will be short.

He'll get out of the car, his legs trembling.

When she sees him, she'll smile. Not because she thinks she has to, or he wants her to. Not nervously, because she doesn't know the rules. Instead, she'll smile at his beauty, and her own roughness. She'll smile because there are new rules now. He won't know these new rules, but she will. They are hers, and she made them for him.

She will cross the road to where he stands, and she will kiss him, and this time, when he cries, she won't let him go.

Many things will happen.

Maybe.

ACKNOWLEDGEMENTS

This has been a long time coming. Six failed novels. Twenty years of trying. And on the way, a lot of people who have had a hand in me not giving up. People who've read early drafts – and other shitter books – and offered just the right level of encouragement (Polly, Spid, Mike, Alex, Chris, Paul, Clare, other Clare, Mark, Andy, Nick, Jacob, Pearl, Mum, Dad, Sue, Rich, other Rich). People who've coped with me flip-flopping between desperately yearning for publication and settling down contentedly into teaching (that's really just you, Clare). People who are endlessly cheerful and full of beans (Joel and Dan). And people whose care, intellectual curiosity, and belief in me has never failed (Mum and Dad).

Then there are the people who gave me the key chances that made a difference, like Josh and Max at Tartaruga, Sam at Galley Beggar, Katie at Liars League, and of course Stefan and Tara at And Other Stories. The people who helped the book along the way – Jeremy for a brilliant job of editing a naïve first-timer, Bella for copy-editing, Jon for a great cover design and Nicky for publicity. The judges of the Northern Book Prize, and the person I was interviewing for a job at the time I got the email, and who must have been quite disconcerted by me shouting 'Fuck, yes!'

There are the people I've worked with, at every school I've taught in (although a special shout out to the English departments – always the true heart of a school, whatever Maths say). Teaching kids is incredible, such a joy, although they are right little gits sometimes.

And lastly, the people I've taught. I didn't understand adolescence when I went through it myself, but watching you lot grow up has been an education, and a privilege. I hope some of you read this. I know the ones I want to the most probably won't, and I find that heartbreaking.

But you're not forgotten.

Dear readers,

As well as relying on bookshop sales, And Other Stories relies on subscriptions from people like you for many of our books, whose stories other publishers often consider too risky to take on.

Our subscribers don't just make the books physically happen. They also help us approach booksellers, because we can demonstrate that our books already have readers and fans. And they give us the security to publish in line with our values, which are collaborative, imaginative and 'shamelessly literary'.

All of our subscribers:

- receive a first-edition copy of each of the books they subscribe to
- are thanked by name at the end of our subscriber-supported books
- receive little extras from us by way of thank you, for example: postcards created by our authors

BECOME A SUBSCRIBER, OR GIVE A SUBSCRIPTION TO A FRIEND

Visit andotherstories.org/subscriptions to help make our books happen. You can subscribe to books we're in the process of making. To purchase books we have already published, we urge you to support your local or favourite bookshop and order directly from them – the often unsung heroes of publishing.

OTHER WAYS TO GET INVOLVED

If you'd like to know about upcoming events and reading groups (our foreign-language reading groups help us choose books to publish, for example) you can:

- join our mailing list at: andotherstories.org
- follow us on Twitter: @andothertweets
- join us on Facebook: facebook.com/AndOtherStoriesBooks
- admire our books on Instagram: @andotherpics
- follow our blog: andotherstories.org/ampersand

CURRENT & UPCOMING BOOKS

01 Juan Pablo Villalobos, *Down the Rabbit Hole*, trans. Rosalind Harvey

02 Clemens Meyer, *All the Lights*, trans. Katy Derbyshire

03 Deborah Levy, *Swimming Home*

04 Iosi Havilio, *Open Door*, trans. Beth Fowler

05 Oleg Zaionchkovsky, *Happiness is Possible*, trans. Andrew Bromfield

06 Carlos Gamerro, *The Islands*, trans. Ian Barnett

07 Christoph Simon, *Zbinden's Progress*, trans. Donal McLaughlin

08 Helen DeWitt, *Lightning Rods*

09 Deborah Levy, *Black Vodka: ten stories*

10 Oleg Pavlov, *Captain of the Steppe*, trans. Ian Appleby

11 Rodrigo de Souza Leão, *All Dogs are Blue*, trans. Zoë Perry and Stefan Tobler

12 Juan Pablo Villalobos, *Quesadillas*, trans. Rosalind Harvey

13 Iosi Havilio, *Paradises*, trans. Beth Fowler

14 Ivan Vladislavić, *Double Negative*

15 Benjamin Lytal, *A Map of Tulsa*

16 Ivan Vladislavić, *The Restless Supermarket*

17 Elvira Dones, *Sworn Virgin*, trans. Clarissa Botsford

18 Oleg Pavlov, *The Matiushin Case*, trans. Andrew Bromfield

19 Paulo Scott, *Nowhere People*, trans. Daniel Hahn

20 Deborah Levy, *An Amorous Discourse in the Suburbs of Hell*

21 Juan Tomás Ávila Laurel, *By Night the Mountain Burns*, trans. Jethro Soutar

22 SJ Naudé, *The Alphabet of Birds*, trans. the author

23 Niyati Keni, *Esperanza Street*

24 Yuri Herrera, *Signs Preceding the End of the World*, trans. Lisa Dillman

25 Carlos Gamerro, *The Adventure of the Busts of Eva Perón*, trans. Ian Barnett

26 Anne Cuneo, *Tregian's Ground*, trans. Roland Glasser and Louise Rogers Lalaurie

27 Angela Readman, *Don't Try This at Home*

28 Ivan Vladislavić, *101 Detectives*

29 Oleg Pavlov, *Requiem for a Soldier*, trans. Anna Gunin

30 Haroldo Conti, *Southeaster*, trans. Jon Lindsay Miles

31 Ivan Vladislavić, *The Folly*

32 Susana Moreira Marques, *Now and at the Hour of Our Death*, trans. Julia Sanches

33 Lina Wolff, *Bret Easton Ellis and the Other Dogs*, trans. Frank Perry

34 Anakana Schofield, *Martin John*

35 Joanna Walsh, *Vertigo*

36 Wolfgang Bauer, *Crossing the Sea*, trans. Sarah Pybus with photographs by Stanislav Krupař

37 Various, *Lunatics, Lovers and Poets: Twelve Stories after Cervantes and Shakespeare*

38 Yuri Herrera, *The Transmigration of Bodies*, trans. Lisa Dillman

39 César Aira, *The Seamstress and the Wind*, trans. Rosalie Knecht

40 Juan Pablo Villalobos, *I'll Sell You a Dog*, trans. Rosalind Harvey

41 Enrique Vila-Matas, *Vampire in Love*, trans. Margaret Jull Costa

42 Emmanuelle Pagano, *Trysting*, trans. Jennifer Higgins and Sophie Lewis

43 Arno Geiger, *The Old King in His Exile*, trans. Stefan Tobler

44 Michelle Tea, *Black Wave*

45 César Aira, *The Little Buddhist Monk*, trans. Nick Caistor

46 César Aira, *The Proof*, trans. Nick Caistor

47 Patty Yumi Cottrell, *Sorry to Disrupt the Peace*

48 Yuri Herrera, *Kingdom Cons*, trans. Lisa Dillman

49 Fleur Jaeggy, *I am the Brother of XX*, trans. Gini Alhadeff

50 Iosi Havilio, *Petite Fleur*, trans. Lorna Scott Fox

51 Juan Tomás Ávila Laurel, *The Gurugu Pledge*, trans. Jethro Soutar

52 Joanna Walsh, *Worlds from the Word's End*
53 Nicola Pugliese, *Malacqua*, trans. Shaun Whiteside
54 César Aira, *The Lime Tree*, trans. Chris Andrews
55 Ann Quin, *The Unmapped Country*
56 Fleur Jaeggy, *Sweet Days of Discipline*, trans. Tim Parks
57 Alicia Kopf, *Brother in Ice*, trans. Mara Faye Lethem
58 Christine Schutt, *Pure Hollywood*
59 Cristina Rivera Garza, *The Iliac Crest*, trans. Sarah Booker
60 Norah Lange, *People in the Room*, trans. Charlotte Whittle
61 Kathy Page, *Dear Evelyn*
62 Alia Trabucco Zerán, *The Remainder*, trans. Sophie Hughes
63 Amy Arnold, *Slip of a Fish*
64 Rita Indiana, *Tentacle*, trans. Achy Obejas
65 Angela Readman, *Something Like Breathing*
66 Gerald Murnane, *Border Districts*
67 Gerald Murnane, *Tamarisk Row*
68 César Aira, *Birthday*, trans. Chris Andrews
69 Ann Quin, *Berg*
70 Fleur Jaeggy, *Proleterka*, trans. Alastair McEwen
71 Olivia Rosenthal, *To Leave with the Reindeer*, trans. Sophie Lewis
72 Lina Wolff, *The Polyglot Lovers*, trans. Saskia Vogel
73 Mario Levrero, *Empty Words*, trans. Annie McDermott
74 Michelle Tea, *Against Memoir*
75 Cristina Rivera Garza, *The Taiga Syndrome*, trans. Suzanne Jill Levine and Aviva Kana
76 Hanne Ørstavik, *Love*, trans. Martin Aitken
77 Tim Etchells, *Endland*
78 Rita Indiana, *Made in Saturn*, trans. Sydney Hutchinson
79 Luke Brown, *Theft*
80 Gerald Murnane, *Collected Short Fiction*
81 Gerald Murnane, *Invisible Yet Enduring Lilacs*
82 James Attlee, *Isolarion*
83 Deb Olin Unferth, *Barn 8*
84 Juan Pablo Villalobos, *I Don't Expect Anyone to Believe Me*, trans. Daniel Hahn
85 Andrzej Tichý, *Wretchedness*, trans. Nichola Smalley
86 Yuri Herrera, *A Silent Fury: The El Bordo Mine Fire*, trans. Lisa Dillman
87 Lina Wolff, *Many People Die Like You*, trans. Saskia Vogel
88 Ann Quin, *Three*
89 Rachel Genn, *What You Could Have Won*
90 John Metcalf, *Medals and Prizes*
91 Claudia Hernández, *Slash and Burn*, trans. Julia Sanches
92 Ann Quin, *Passages*
93 Various, *This Is How We Come Back Stronger*
94 Eva Baltasar, *Permafrost*, trans. Julia Sanches
95 Norah Lange, *Notes from Childhood*, trans. Charlotte Whittle
96 James Attlee, *Under the Rainbow: Voices from the First Lockdown*
97 César Aira, *The Divorce*, trans. Chris Andrews
98 Mario Levrero, *The Luminous Novel*, trans. Annie McDermott
99 Tice Cin, *Keeping the House*
100 Yuri Herrera, *Three Novels*, trans. Lisa Dillman
101 Elisa Victoria, *Oldladyvoice*, trans. Charlotte Whittle
102 Sammy Wright, *Fit*
103 Robin McLean, *Pity the Beast*
104 Mona Arshi, *Somebody Loves You*

SAMMY WRIGHT is a teacher. He was brought up in Edinburgh, worked in London for twelve years, and now lives in Newcastle. He is a member of the Social Mobility Commission and is currently vice principal of a large secondary school in Sunderland. His short stories have been published in a variety of anthologies and his novel *Fit*, which won the 2020 Northern Book Prize, is his first book-length publication.